MATH

)

Y

LIER

Thank You For Your Purchase
Great reviews mean everything to a writer. If you enjoyed this eBook in any way, please take a moment and go to Amazon and let me, and other readers, know what you thought. Once again, thank you and enjoy!

Kai's Aftermath

© 2011 by K. Elle Collier

product of the author's imagination or are used fictitiously.

ISBN – 13: 978-0-9816495-4-2

Penticle Publishing
Studio City, CA 91602

Cover Design by Tamara Ramsay

More books by K. Elle Collier

My Man's Best Friend (Book 1)

Alana Bites Back (Book 3) – Coming 2013

Intimate Stranger –(New Novel) Coming 2013

Are you ready to write a novel? Pick up...

From Concept to Kindle:
A Step-by-Step to Writing, Publishing and
Marketing your Novel on the Amazon Kindle

For more tips and a bunch of great stuff visit:

www.modernwritingworks.com

http://www.kellecollier.com/

Follow me on Twitter @K_ElleCollier
Like me on Facebook: Author K. Elle Collier

"Writing is a dance with words, you start off slow and
build to a beautiful rhythmic flow".

~K. Elle

CHAPTER 1

KAI

I realized the moment I stepped off the plane at JFK that my life was never going to be the same again. I haven't felt like myself since my doctor told me I was pregnant, or "knocked up" as my best friend Simone refers to it. Todd and I had been apart for less than a month when I found out I was expecting his child. I wondered if I was running away from my past, but I didn't care. I needed a change, a fresh start, something to get me focused and thinking about a new game plan, as well as the whole new life ahead of me.

As I stood in the Delta terminal, I suddenly realized that I was about to be somebody's mother with no man for me or father for the baby. Of course that might all change once Todd finds out that we had a child on the way - but, when he found out, I wanted to be sure it was done at just the right time and in just the right way. But even then, I wouldn't hold my breath on him wanting to be in my life again, or even be a part of this baby's life. Then again, I may not want him back. The bottom line was I had made a lot of mistakes in my life and, well, now I was paying for them. I knew it was wrong to have an affair with Alana, Todd's best friend. But what I didn't know was that Alana had a plan of her own, one that included finding out that Alana's daughter was actually Alana and Todd's daughter, a fact that eventually led Todd to choose her over me, a fact that hurt more than life itself. Yep, Alana had a master plan from the very beginning to make Todd hers. A plan filled with deceit and betrayal, two words that turned my life upside down without so much as a warning or a smoke signal. But now it's my turn to do some damage.

When Alana sees me coming her way, pregnant with Todd's baby, the look on her face will be one that I won't want to miss and will definitely capture for posterity. But like I had told her once before, she may have won the battle by stealing Todd away from me, but the war wasn't close to being over, because this time, I, Kai Edwards, had a plan of her own and I was in it to win it.

So there I stood, in New York City, my new home, after leaving Chicago, Todd and Alana behind to start a new life. I took a deep breath as I headed toward the baggage claim. As I turned on my cell phone, it rang within seconds. I looked down to see it was my best friend Simone calling.

"You must have some sort of tracking device on me, I just walked off the plane," I said, smiling from ear to ear. I had only been in New York for five minutes and I already missed Simone.

"Of course I do," Simone said. "How was your flight?"

"Nice and quick, just like I like it," I said, thinking how that must have sounded.

"Good. You should have a car waiting for you to take you to your place." Simone's tone softened as the question I expected came, "So how are you feeling?"

"A little morning sickness at times but I'm sure that comes with the territory."

"Believe me," Simone replied, "you have no idea. Wait until your ankles are the same size as your knees and you can't even see your vajayjay to do any type of updating, if you know what I mean. Then, my friend, you know you're pregnant."

"Thanks, Simone, I so look forward to that." I paused, suddenly conscious that I was having an intimate moment with my best friend in the middle of JFK airport.

"Simone, do you think I'm doing the right thing? I mean, having this baby and all, especially since Todd is no longer in my life?"

"Absolutely. You finding out that you were pregnant was nothing short of a blessing. Remember, you never thought you could have kids, something that eventually made Todd pick that witch Alana over you. Moving to New York on the other hand, well, that remains to be seen. The good news is, you can always come back home to Chicago."

"Yeah, this is true," I said, feeling relief wash over me.

"Give New York a run for its money," Simone continued, "and if it's not the fit you're expecting, you've always got a job back here at McKenzie and Strong."

"Thanks, Simone. Hey, gotta go, I'm going to call you later."

"Of course, love you," Simone said.

"You too."

I ended my call and walked through the double glass doors into the baggage claim letting what Simone had said roll through my head. As I entered the crowd of people waiting to pick up their baggage, my eyes were diverted to a short, plump white man wearing a black trench coat and white shirt, black slacks and shiny black shoes holding a sign with my name on it, Kai Edwards. Simone had arranged for a car to pick me up at the airport and I was truly thankful for that, especially since I still had to make my way to Brooklyn, where my new home and new way of life was waiting for me. I'd only been to Brooklyn a few times before, but one thing I can say about that culturally diverse place is that I love every inch of it. From the parks and the quaint cafés to the beautiful architecture and multitude of breathtaking brownstones, Brooklyn had a feel like no other in New York.

I nodded to the driver who spotted me immediately as he quickly proceeded towards me to assist with my baggage. I love being catered to, especially when I am in a city that I am not too familiar with. It's just one less thing to worry about.

We headed outside to the cold air of New York. It was nearing twilight and the temperature was a brisk 40 degrees. The best part about New York was the energy that infused the air around you – it was different and more powerful than any other city in the world. The people, the smell, and the grit, along with the vibrant lights, just screamed, "I am a city to be reckoned with."

I dipped my head into the black Town Car and settled in the backseat as the driver closed my door behind me. He quickly moved to his seat and started the car. Soon, we were headed up the Jackie Robinson Parkway to Atlantic Avenue, which after a few short moments, dropped us into our destination, Fort Green, Brooklyn. We cruised down Adelphi Street until turning onto South Oxford Street and pulled up to my new place. I gazed out the taxi window to see my new home, a three story beautiful brick brownstone with large picture bay windows.

I found out during my 30-minute ride that my plump little driver goes by "Albert." He wasn't the chattiest guy, but I found that refreshing since my objective on the ride to Fort Green was to get a little shuteye.

Albert opened the back door and I stepped out to a beautiful tree-lined street. Cars were packed like sardines on the quaint little block and I soaked in the neighborhood, getting used to my new home. I headed up the front stairs of my new building and noticed the brownstone was divided into three individual apartments - the basement level and the first and second floors. The second floor apartment was actually two levels and the biggest of the three where the owner of the brownstone lived.

The advertising firm I was working for found this place for me and I was so very grateful. Finding a decent place to live in New York – even in Brooklyn can be a taxing ordeal, stress I really didn't need at the moment.

The Firm informed me that the brownstone was convenient to all transportation as well as cafés, restaurants and other small boutiques. Since I was working in Manhattan(Soho to be exact), I was also told that the best way to get to work was by jumping on the train, where I had a choice of taking either the "2", the "3" or the "C" from Fort Green directly into Soho. Can't beat that I thought to myself.

I was feeling a little tired after my journey and, as always these days, hungry. Being two months pregnant can take a lot out of you. Sleeping (already one of my hobbies) has become my favorite pastime - next to eating, of course. Although if the morning sickness would just subside, I think I would be a happier woman.

Albert grabbed my bags from the trunk and we headed up to my new apartment. I pulled out the keys that had been mailed to me last month and entered my new abode. Upon entering the foyer, I stepped in a few more feet and found myself standing in an exquisite, open living room with cherry wood floors and vaulted ceilings.

I hit the switch on the wall and saw the beautiful floors was just the beginning. I stood there for a moment and took in the whole scene, and just enjoyed the moment – my new place was truly breathtaking.

One of the reasons I love brownstones so much is that they have so much character and style. Handcrafted molding lined the ceiling and the brick fireplace scaled the eight-foot wall from floor to ceiling. I moved past the living room and headed into the dining room, noting how nicely they flowed together. To the right of the dining room was the kitchen, and to the left of it was the bedroom. The kitchen looked as if it had been newly remodeled with a brownish gold granite countertop and light maple overlay cabinets. The kitchen floor was a reddish brown Spanish tile and the appliances were all state of the art stainless steel. The best thing about the place (other than it being absolutely perfect), was that it came furnished with everything I might need. I signaled to Albert to put my bags into my bedroom and he did so promptly. I reached into my coat pocket and pulled out a 20-dollar bill, sliding it into his pudgy right hand. He smiled and nodded at me as he turned to leave, letting himself out.

As I walked back through the dining room and into the living room I saw a shadow approaching my front door, followed by a soft knock. I couldn't imagine who that could have been, so I approached the door cautiously and looked through the decorative glass. The person looking at me from the other side gave me an inviting smile and I smiled back as I opened the door to greet her.

"You must be Kai," the woman said with a huge warm smile.

"I am."

"I'm Toni, I live right above you."

"Oh, you must be the owner of the building," I said.

"You could say that, but I don't go around boasting about it." Toni chuckled.

"Please come in," I said quickly and opened the door to allow Toni to enter.

"How was your flight?" Toni asked as we stood in the foyer, about three feet apart.

"It was great," I replied, "no complaints here."

"Right on," Toni said with a huge smile. I was struck by the fact that I hadn't heard someone use that phrase since the seventies.

"Well, I don't want to be a bother, I know you must be tired and want to settle in. I just wanted to come by and say 'hello' and welcome you to New York," Toni continued.

"Well, thank you so much," I said, feeling a sense of comfort with her. Toni was a caramel-colored woman with blond dreads and an electrifying smile. She was a little on the thicker side, but not fat. With her oversized button-up shirt and faded jeans with wool socks stuffed into a grey pair of crocks, Toni was the quintessential Brooklynite.

"Well, I live right upstairs and if you ever need anything, please do not hesitate to come knock on my door."

"Thanks, I will. And by the way, your building is lovely," I said, still admiring my new dwelling.

"Thank you, I try to keep it presentable, it was a gift from my grandfather years ago. A college gift you might call it."

"That was very nice of him," I said.

"Well," Toni said a little slowly, "at the time I didn't think so, especially since he gave my brother a brand new car and I got an old building, but looks like I came out on top."

"I would say so."

"I don't want to keep you, so holler if you need anything," Toni said.

"I will, thank you."

Toni left and I closed the door behind her, locking the two deadbolts on the door. I flicked off the living room lamp and headed to my bedroom to unpack.

Yep, I thought to myself, this may work out just fine.

CHAPTER 2
ALANA

Men kill me. I mean, let's be real, Todd thinks it's just dandy that we live in the same condo that he and Kai shared, but it's just plain stupid, so he can get over it because it's not gonna happen.

His philosophy was, "Baby, I know Kai and I used to live here together but this is our place now." Yeah, right, not gonna fly with me, not at 'tall. I quickly whipped out my Blackberry and scrolled through my to-do list, and saw the note saying it was time for us to look for a new place - one that didn't have Kai residue all over it. A place that I could call ours. I'm sure once Todd sees this as getting a clean start on our relationship, he won't fight me on this and quickly come around. Besides, by the look of his condo, I know we can do so much better than this place. Plus, I like to think I have better taste than Kai anyway.

After adding a few more items in my to-do list, I scrolled over to my daily planner and saw I had my first photo shoot with Victoria's Secret next week. Landing that Victoria's Secret gig gave me just the smallest hint of what will become of my career. I laughed at how it all started with Kai giving me a job as a model at her advertising firm. It couldn't have worked out more perfectly when it came to the bigger scheme of things.

Now, I did have to eat a little pussy along the way, but sometimes you had to take one for the team as I like to say. In the end I got the man and I have the family and soon I will have the booming career, too. Life couldn't be any better right now. The next step is marriage and that won't be too hard, especially since Todd and I have a 'child' together now. I can't wait to see the look on Kai's face when she sees that big fat ring on my finger, and believe me, it will be PHAT because Alana doesn't do small.

I did have to be careful, to not reveal the secret that could ruin everything, and reveal much more than

I could handle, or spin in my favor. But the fact was, I am careful, very careful. Everything should run smoothly from here on out. Kai is finally out of our lives and if I have anything to do with it, out for good.

My cell phone rang and I noticed it was my agent, so I stopped what I was doing to take his call.

"Emanuel! How are you, sweetie?" I sang as I answered. My mother always used to say to smile when you answer the phone because the person on the other end can always hear it in your voice.

Emanuel was the newest addition to my thriving career. He had found me a few months ago and had been relentless until I had signed with him. I had no intentions of going with his company, "The Vaughn Agency," but you have to give it to a man who wouldn't take no for an answer. I later found out that Emanuel was the son of William Vaughn, the founder of the agency and a very rich and powerful man in the entertainment industry. They have offices in New York, California and now Chicago. And I was their latest and greatest new client. Emanuel was calling to tell me about a part in an indie film that he thought I would be perfect for. The director was originally from Chicago, but has done many films while living in Los Angeles, so he knew what he's doing. This new film is based on his life growing up on Chicago's West Side and Emanuel thought I would be perfect for the mistress. I was so thrilled that this director was even interested in using me that I didn't even put up a fight about being the "other woman," not to mention that I was now transitioning my talents into acting.

I told Emanuel that we should meet for drinks to hash this out further. He agreed and said he would messenger over the script to me tonight so I could read it before we met. I was on Cloud Nine. I felt like Halle Berry.

I hung up with Emanuel and dialed Todd's number. I needed to share the news with someone and, of course, Todd was the first person that popped into my head.

Todd picked up the phone as if he were rushing to get somewhere, and I could tell he wasn't smiling as he answered, until I realized that he always sounded like that.

"Hey, baby, you busy?" I asked with a huge smile on my face.

"Always, but what's up?" he answered curtly.

"You have any plans tonight?"

"Not really."

"Good," I said, "Because we are going to dinner, to celebrate."

"What are we celebrating?" Todd asked in a pre-occupied voice as I heard him shuffling papers on his desk.

"It's a surprise, but I will tell you all about it tonight."

There was a long pause and the papers stopped rustling. "Are you pregnant – again?" Todd asked, in a half playful, half serious tone.

"Ah, no," I said, and I heard the slight sigh of relief on the other end of the line.

"Well, give a brother a small hint," he pleaded.

"Nope, you will just have to wait till later."

"Fine. Baby I gotta run, but text me with the time and place and I will meet you."

"I will," I promised. "See you tonight."

I hung up the phone and dialed my real estate agent. No better time than the present to start looking for our new place. I felt like Weezie on that old TV show, The Jeffersons. I'm moving on up!

CHAPTER 3
TODD

My day was flying by, I glanced at my watch to see that it was already 4:30pm. I realized I had to finish up as I had to meet Alana for dinner at six. I was typing up the last of some briefs when my partner Maceo entered my office. Maceo Smith was a brother from the hood with book smarts to boot. I met him in law school where we and we hit it off instantly. He was a no-nonsense type guy and I liked his tactics in and out of the courtroom. So when I thought about opening my own practice, he was the first person that popped into my head. To my surprise he jumped at the opportunity, he had been looking for a way to get out of the rat race and those big stuffy law firms.

"What up, what up?" Maceo said as he walked in my office with his trademark swagger and sat down across from me. Maceo was a very attractive man with a bald head and goatee. His chiseled features made him a great candidate for modeling, something he had done while in Law School to help pay the bills, though, his real dream was to become a litigator.

"Maceo, my main man, tell me something good," I said. I always felt the need to incorporate slang when I interacted one on one with Maceo, though I'm not sure if he would have considered any part of my vocabulary slang.

"Yo, just got out of court and had a slam dunk with the Williams case. Did you know that bitch actually thought she could pull 500 thou from our client?" Maceo boasted.

"Yeah, the Misses was out for blood. So what was the final payoff?" I asked.

"50 thou and a fucking Happy Meal. And I dare her whack ass lawyer to try to appeal. Women fucking kill me," Maceo said, brushing his right leg as if trying to get lint off his pants.

"Well, you gotta give her some credit for thinking she could try to get that much out of our client."

"Well, she can think that all she wants, Miss 'I-sit-on-my-ass-all-day-while-shopping-and-drinking-martini's-with-my-friends' is gonna have to get a real damn job."

I chuckled at Maceo's recap. I knew he had been the right guy for this case. "Well, good work," I said and looked back at my paperwork doing my level best to finish it, he wasn't the only one with a case to try in the morning.

"So, you want to go grab a few brews after work?"

"I can't," I replied. "I have to meet Alana for dinner, apparently she has something she wants to tell me."

"So how is that going? Dating the best friend and all?" Maceo asked with a slight grin forming across his face.

"It's going, but to be honest, she is very different than Kai. A little more demanding, but that can be refreshing at times."

Maceo scrunched up his face like he just bit into a nice ripe lemon. "Refreshing? When in the hell has a demanding woman ever been refreshing, yo?"

I really didn't know how to answer that. I guess my definition of refreshing was a bit different than Maceo's.

"Let me tell you, I dated this dime piece for a minute and she had the nerve to tell me when and what time I could come over and fuck her. Me, Maceo Smith."

"So what did you do?"

"Oh," he answered, "I obliged her, Maceo doesn't pass up tappin' that ass, but you'd best believe she got the infamous voicemail from then on out. You only get one shot to make a good impression with Maceo."

I couldn't help but laugh at Maceo's antics and his numerous stories about his misadventures with women. If I had not seen him with my very own eyes in the courtroom, I wouldn't have believed that he could actually incorporate his street smarts with his law school education and come off sounding educated and professional – in the courtroom, that is. Outside of court, that was a whole other scenario.

"Was that the doctor?" I asked.

"Naw, the investment banker."

"What happened to the doctor?" I asked.

"I don't even want to talk about that crazy bitch," he said. "I should have snapped her neck when I had the chance. But listen, I don't want to interrupt you. I see you have business to take care of before you meet the little lady, so I will hit you before I'm out."

"Sounds good. Nice work today."

"Nothin' but a notion, my brother." Maceo said as he stood.

And with that, Maceo swaggered out my office just as smoothly as he had swaggered in.

CHAPTER 4
TODD

I arrived at Table 5 and realized I had beaten Alana there, as usual. Alana was always running late. It didn't matter if she was a bystander or the guest of honor. Alana would arrive when Alana was ready. It hadn't bothered me when we were "just friends," but now that we'd taken our relationship to the so-called 'next level,' yeah, her tardiness kinda gets under my skin a bit. But I'm a man, and smart men know when to pick their battles - this was one of those times when it's best to stay off the battlefield. Ever since Alana had moved to Chicago a year ago (and into the middle of my relationship with Kai), my simple (and some would call boring) life had become much more turbulent. As a divorce lawyer I see most of my excitement in the courtroom, not in my own personal life, and that's usually how I like to keep it. But things change, especially when you factor in how your fiancé was not only cheating on you, but cheating with your best 'female' friend. Shit just isn't the same and that boring life I once led is now a 60-minute episode of Law and Order.

Alana finally arrived, 15 minutes late. I was already seated when she walked in so the hostess escorted her in my direction. I would have waited to start drinking with her but it had been a long day at the office, which had included two preliminary hearings back to back. Needless to say, I needed something to take the edge off. As I watched Alana walk toward me I couldn't help but notice how damn sexy she looked. It never ceases to amaze me that whatever Alana puts on, she looks good, and tonight was no exception. She wore a form fitting ribbed light pink tank top with a matching pink paisley skirt that stopped mid thigh and hugged her hips ever so nicely. I never really noticed before just how sexy Alana was – OK, I'm lying through my damn teeth, but when I was with Kai, I didn't look at Alana that way as much. I was content with Kai, she kept me satisfied and now that she is gone, well, now my full attention is on Alana. Watching Alana approach, I started to think of a few other things I could use to take the edge off right about now, but I held that thought for later.

"Hey, baby," Alana said as she planted a soft kiss on my lips. She smelled good. "I know I'm late but I had to finish up a call. Are you mad?" Alana asked as she sat down across from me.

"Nope, but I do expect some compensatory damages for making me wait," I said in my most seductive manner.

Alana leaned up on her elbows, and threw on her most seductive smile. "And what do you propose, counselor?

"Well, for starters, a little extra attention later on." I said.

"And if I decline?"

"Well, then I will just have to file an appeal," I said.

We continued to stare into each other's eyes, before we both laughed at our silly seductive role-play.

"So," I asked, "what's the big news that you had to meet for dinner instead of talking at home?" I had been hoping to turn in early that night, but when Alana wanted something, Alana kept pushing until she got it.

"Well, I have some very exciting news, baby, and I wanted to celebrate with you!" Alana said as she beamed from ear to ear.

"Well, what is it?" I asked again. "And please don't make me guess, I am not in the mood for that."

"Oh, you suck at that anyway."

"What?" I said feeling a bit offended at Alana's assessment of my guessing ability.

"Kidding," she said. "OK, so remember how a few months ago I got a call about maybe doing a movie?"

"Of course."

"Well, they called yesterday and want me to be in a new indie film shooting right here in Chicago. Me? Can you believe it?" Alana asked. "I didn't think it would happen so fast, right?" Alana said in an overly excited tone.

"Wow, that is great!" I exclaimed. "You're going to be in a movie?"

"Yep."

"On the big screen?"

"Yep."

"Damn baby," I said, grinning, "that's amazing!"

"Well, I am one amazing bitch!" Alana said as she smiled from ear to ear.

"I think we should order another bottle of wine to celebrate," I said.

"I could think of a few things we could do to celebrate," Alana replied with a seductive wink.

"Damn, you must be reading my mind," I said with a smile.

"One of my more popular traits. Order that wine, I'm gonna go to the ladies' room."

"Coming right up," I said.

***

As Todd flagged down our waitress, I headed toward the back of the restaurant. Halfway to the bathroom I noticed a woman staring at me, the same woman that had been staring at me when I walked into the restaurant, and the same woman who had continued to stare at me while I dined with Todd.

I walked past her table and she gave me a small smile. I returned her pleasant gesture and kept on moving towards the bathroom.

In the bathroom, as I began to touch up my makeup I noticed a few women entering, three to be exact, and the last one was the woman I exchanged pleasantries with a just a few minutes before.

The woman entered the restroom but did not enter a stall, but stood a few feet away from me adjusting her clothing before proceeding to play with her hair, shooting a few glances at me. I looked away, then back at her, and noticed she was staring.

"Do I know you?" I asked.

"Why do you ask?" the woman replied, her voice was strong and confident.

"Maybe because you've been staring at me the whole time I've been here."

"Well," she said, "you're a very beautiful woman."

Of course I am, I wanted to say, but I have learned that some things are better left unspoken.

"Thank you," I said.

The woman stepped a few feet closer to me and extended her hand, "My name is Jessica, Jessica McCoy." Jessica was a striking looking woman with a short Halle Berry cut that looked as if she just stepped out of the beauty salon, there wasn't one strand of hair out of place. Her skin was a silky dark chocolate and she was a bit on the thick side, but she wore it well. The thing that really stood out about Jessica to me was her teeth. They were the whitest and straightest teeth I had ever seen, and the way she smiled from ear to ear, I'm sure she was very aware of her thirty two pearly assets. "Nice to meet you, Jessica," I said.

"And you are?"

"Alana Brooks."

"The pleasure is mine, Alana Brooks."

"Right," I said. I finished up, taking a final glance at myself in the mirror before I began to head out of the bathroom. Jessica continued to talk, catching my attention once again.

"I'm new in town, just moved here from New York," Jessica said. "Job transfer."

"I see," I said, responding with not a trace of enthusiasm in my voice.

"Maybe we can hang out sometime," she said, "and you can show me the city."

I stopped and turned around, thinking that was pretty bold of her, seeing that I just met her five seconds earlier. But there was no need to be a bitch about her sudden desire for me to be her Chicago tour guide.

I took a very polite tone with this Jessica woman. "I'm a busy woman so that probably wouldn't work for me."

"Well, if you change your mind here's my information," Jessica said as she extended her business card my way. I looked at it briefly before taking it, out of pure politeness, of course. I smiled, looking down at the black print.

"Hmm, assistant district attorney," I murmured. "Impressive."

"I think so," Jessica said.

"Well, Jessica the ADA, welcome to Chicago and although I am flattered by your subtle advances, I think you failed to see one minor detail."

"Which is?" Jessica asked with a smile.

"I have a man."

Jessica looked me up and down then connected with me with her eyes. "Of course you do. That's why I gave you my card."

Jessica smiled then passed me as she headed out of the bathroom. "You have a good night," she said.

I stood there for a minute trying to figure out what had just happened, and I wasn't sure if I liked what just went down. I threw her card on the counter and headed out the door, back to my date with Todd.

***

As I poured the wine from the new bottle that I had just ordered, I noticed Alana heading back to our table. I couldn't help but to notice how confident she looked as she strutted across the restaurant.

"What took you so long?" I asked. I slid her newly filled glass toward Alana as she sat back down across from me.

"Oh, I ran into an old friend in the bathroom," she replied. "You know how that is."

"A friend from school?"

"No."

"Another Victoria Secret model?"

"No, honey, just a friend I met through a friend." Alana smiled, but she looked uncomfortable and quickly glanced at something behind her.

"Oh, OK," I said as I picked up my glass of wine.

Alana turned again and looked across the room, staring at something or someone, so much that I turned around to see what she was looking at. Alana's gaze led me to a woman, sitting at a table with some nondescript guy.

"Is that your friend?" I asked.

"Um, who?"

"That woman who's staring at you," I answered. "Quite seductively, I should add. Is there something you need to tell me?" I couldn't believe what I was seeing, Alana was flirting with another woman while at dinner with me.

"Are you flirting with her?" I asked.

"Baby, please!" Alana protested.

"Well," I said, "don't act like it would be a first or anything."

"OK, fine, she made a pass at me in the bathroom, but I told her I was here with my man and I don't get down like that."

"Any more, you mean."

"What?" she asked.

"You meant to say, you don't get down like that any more."

"Whatever, Todd. Are we gonna go there?"

"Ah, apparently we should, Alana," I replied. "I'm not going to go down the same damn road as I did with Kai."

"Listen, baby," she said, "If I ever get with another woman, which is highly doubtful, you would know. Actually, you would be involved."

"Involved in what way?" I asked.

"Like, you know, a threesome," Alana half-whispered.

"Really?" Just hearing that magic word, I felt my penis getting hard. I have never had a threesome before and, although I think it was wrong on many levels what Alana and Kai did behind my back, damn, they could have asked me to join in, at least once.

"You wanna do a threesome baby?" she asked.

"Well, it's not like I don't want to do one," I responded with slight enthusiasm, although trying not to sound like that was the ultimate goal of life.

"OK." Alana smiled at seeing me get a little excited.

"Of course, no strings attached," I added, "and I don't want to come home one day and find you fucking her in our bed. It's all or nothing."

"Please, baby," Alana said. "I told you, that one-on-one lesbian shit is so in my past. But a nice juicy threesome is very much in our future."

Alana glided her foot up my pants leg and began to massage my very hard penis.

"You like her?" Alana said as her eyes drifted over to Jessica, who was now preoccupied with her dinner date. I slowly turned around to catch another glance, a better one.

"She's not bad," I said, "but I think we can do better."

"Is that so? Well, let me look around for 'us' and see what I can wrangle up."

"I like how that sounds," I said.

"Then strap up, cowboy," Alana smiled, "'cause you ain't seen nothin' yet."

****

Todd and I returned back home at around 8:30pm and we were both feeling more than a bit tipsy. I couldn't stop thinking about that woman in the bathroom. Not that I was attracted to her or anything, but just at how aggressive she was. And for her to just assume that I would call her. Well, she can get over that notion. I'm glad I left her card on the counter. Maybe some dyke bitch will see it and call her. That'd serve her ass right.

While Todd was undressing in the bedroom and I stood in the bathroom taking off my makeup. Todd entered the bathroom and turned on the shower. He had stripped down to his black Calvin Klein's and I couldn't help but stare. One thing I always admired about my best friend was that his body was always tight. Todd slipped off his Calvin's as he shot me a look.

"Care to join me?" Todd asked with a sexy smirk on his face.

The temperature in the bathroom was rising and not just from the hot water and steam. I looked down at Todd's manhood and it was standing erect and ready for play.

"I would love to," I said as I finished removing the last of my makeup and slowly stripped down to nothing.

Todd stepped in the shower and began lathering himself up. One thing I noticed about him was that he loved to smell good. That is a very attractive trait in a man.

I waited a few minutes before entering the shower, just to make sure Todd was done with his head to toe soap-and-rinse regimen. I like to work with a clean slate, and not one with "work residue" on it. I stepped in the shower with a plan, a plan to seduce my man, because, hell, it had been a great day so why stop? Todd was facing the shower head as I stepped in behind him and wrapped my arms around his waist to encompass his penis with my right hand.

Yeah, he knew what time it was, and me stroking his manhood was only the beginning. I like to pride myself on knowing that I can pleasure a man with my mouth and mouth only. In fact, I've been told in the

past that I should get business cards made for my
specialty, although I always took that as a pure
compliment, because not just anyone will get the
"Alana treatment."

I turned Todd around and he immediately began to
kiss me, our mouths tasting each other as if it were
the first time. I continued to stroke his manhood
because I knew after our tongues were tired of
dancing in each other's mouths I was headed
downtown to work him out a bit more.

Todd pulled away for a minute and pushed his
mouth against my right ear.

"I want to see you fucking another woman," Todd
said passionately.

I kinda smiled at Todd's adventurous request.

"I wanna watch her tongue in you," he continued.

That sent a small tingle through my body. I
thought to myself, I'm sure that seeing my interaction
with Jessica earlier that night must have sparked this
sudden burst of sexual exploration on his part. Of
course, I was down for whatever, especially if it kept
my man satisfied.

"Whatever you like, baby," I breathed, "I can even
set it up for you."

"Let's do that," Todd said.

See, one thing Kai didn't know was how to satisfy
her man, and one thing I have learned is that men are
simple – fuck 'em, feed 'em and give them that extra

bit of desire to keep them close. Kai fucking me on the side and never letting Todd in on it was a bad idea, though it ended up working out in my best interests, so kudos for me.

"I want her to be just as hot as you," Todd said, "and I want to hear you moan as she eats you." Todd was turning me the hell on and that only made me want to pleasure him even more.

I bent down and began to do what I do best, and yes, I do it well. If a man does not cum within four minutes in my mouth, then we have a problem, a big one. I sucked and stroked Todd's rock hard penis for all of three minutes before he finally came, I felt his body go limp and his penis soften in my mouth. He dropped his head as the water cascaded over him, leaking out small moans of after pleasure. Just a day in the life of Alana Brooks satisfying her man. I stood to see Todd staring at me with a huge satisfied grin on his face.

"Damn, baby, you are so good!"

That's right, I agreed silently, and don't you forget it when your ass tries to stray on me.

"I'm good for you," I said.

Todd then lathered me down and rinsed me off before we both jumped out of the shower and into our bed, where we made love for the next few hours until we both passed out from exhaustion.

CHAPTER 5
KAI

"Alana is just a manipulative bitch, period," I said.

I was in Dr. Caroline Albright's office for my second visit to a therapist. My first visit had been a bit awkward mainly because it had been at least 15 years since the last time I had walked through the doors of a real psychologist. I knew a visit was way overdue, but for some reason I hadn't been ready until then. For years after my traumatic event I always contemplated seeing someone, but I figured my bad dreams would pass. After what my brother, Raymond, sprung on me, it kinda sent me back into a space I knew that I needed help getting out of.

"Is that how you really feel or is that your anger talking?" Dr. Albright asked as she stared at me through her brownish-black Oliver People's glasses. She was an interesting looking woman, with an eccentric style, almost as if she had been caught in a fashion time warp of sorts. So long as she continued to give me good therapy, she could dress from the 1920s all she wanted for all I cared.

I propped myself up on my left elbow to contemplate her question. I wasn't totally sure how I really felt. I realize I am still a bit upset, but my intentions are usually for the best no matter how someone treats me.

"I'm assuming you want the truth?"

"Well," Dr. Albright continued, "isn't that why we are here, to speak our truths?"

I sure hate how therapists answer a question with a question. I wonder if they teach them how to do that in shrink school.

"I hate to admit it," I said, "but you're right. I have to stop kicking myself at how I let that woman get the best of me. I don't know... I just have a lot of emotions swirling in my head right now, so maybe we shouldn't be talking about her."

"Do you want to talk about Todd?"

"No," I said, "Because that will lead to talking about Alana."

Dr. Albright scribbled something down on her little yellow pad and she took a deep breath. I wondered if I was considered a difficult patient. I wondered if she was annoyed with me avoiding the main issue I was there to talk about. She looked back up from her notepad.

"OK, would you like to talk about your brother?"

"Raymond?"

"Yes," Dr. Albright replied.

"What about him?"

"Well, let's start with how you feel about him."

"The fact that he deceived and pawned me off as a toy to some random guys so he could get high, I'd say I'm a bit pissed off." I said. I waited for a reply that didn't come. "I could go on," I volunteered.

·   "Are you sleeping at night?" Dr. Albright asked.

"A little," I answered, "but between being three months pregnant and living in a new city, it's hard sometimes."

"Have you spoken to your brother since you've been in New York?"

"No, and the question you should be asking is; 'do I want to?' Not really."

"You know, Kai, holding on to resentment and anger only hurts you. I know you need time to heal, but forgiveness is also a step toward that."

I knew that Dr. Albright was right, and that I needed to find it in my heart to forgive Raymond for what he'd done. It was just so hard. I still didn't understand why he did what he did. I looked at my watch and realized that I had only a few minutes left, which was probably for the best since I had made it pretty clear I wasn't ready to talk about Alana and Todd.

"Kai, are you with me?" Dr. Albright asked in her soft, comforting voice, pulling me out of my trance.

"Yeah," I replied, "I'm here."

"Before our time is up, did you want to touch upon that day when you were younger? The day the traumatic event happened that you blame your brother for?"

I turned from my side and lay flat on my back, staring at the ceiling. It was light blue with splashes of white speckles in it. I wondered if turning off all the lights made the speckles glow.

"No, I think we should wait until maybe next time," I finally said as I shifted toward her with a smile.

"OK, that's fine," Dr. Albright said as she scribbled in her notepad again. I lay very still as if my moving would have interrupted her flow.

"Kai, I recommend long, warm baths before bed to relax your body. Being three months pregnant," she went on, "you don't want to stress out your body, as it's not good for the baby."

"Yes, the baby," I said, "how could I forget?"

"Kai, I have to be honest," Dr. Albright continued. "I'm a little worried about you. Being in a strange new city along with being pregnant, and starting a new job, too. Do you have any family here, anyone that you can lean on?"

"No, not really," I answered, "but I'll be OK. I adapt pretty easily. Besides, I met this very nice woman who owns my building, so that's one person." I sat up and smoothed out out my hair. I looked at Dr. Albright, who had removed her glasses. She looked a lot less intimidating without them. "Thanks for your concern," I said finally, smiling at her.

"Make sure you schedule your next appointment with my assistant.Let's try for next Friday if you can."

"Okey dokey, doc." I hated how that sounded before it even escaped my lips, although Dr. Albright gave me a broad grin upon hearing it.

"Great, take care of yourself, Kai."

"I will."

I headed out of Dr. Albright's office and down South Elliott Place. I loved that I could walk everywhere in New York. My house was only a few blocks away from her office, so I looked at this as a regular dose of exercise.

I felt good about my second visit. I wasn't sure how long I would continue to go, but for now, it was a good start.

CHAPTER 6
ALANA

I needed to get a cup of coffee. I was on a mission. I headed into Aroma Café and was pleasantly surprised that there was no line. I pranced up to the counter and ordered a double chai latte, pronto, my newest obsession. I stepped to the side to wait for my fix and whipped out my Blackberry while I went over my agenda for the day. Hair and make-up for a shoot at noon, Victoria's Secret fitting at three and dinner with my agent at seven. My days were nothing but busy and I was starting to get a bit overwhelmed. But as my agent, Emanuel bluntly let me know, my heyday wouldn't last forever and soon I would wake up to a phone that had stopped ringing. He can be so blunt, but I love his honesty.

I scooped up my chai latte and headed toward the exit when I bumped into a woman entering Aroma Café. I look up and noticed it was that Jessica woman from the restaurant. Shit!

"Hey, beautiful," Jessica said with a broad smile. "What a surprise running into you."

"That it is," I said with a flat tone.

We stepped aside to let some other people enter the café. I then walked a few feet away from the door to be out of earshot of anyone lingering around.

"So how are you?" Jessica said in a conversational way.

"Pretty busy."

"I'm sure. Oh, by the way, I wanted to give this to you again. You must have forgotten it in the bathroom the other night."

I looked down to see that Jessica was giving me yet another business card.

"Yeah, I kinda did that on purpose."

"And why would you do that?" she asked.

"Because I told you, Jessica, I have a man."

"Oh, right, you did mention that."

"Yeah, a few times," I said emphasizing few.

"Yeah, right, right. You did happen to mention that." Jessica said smiling looking me up and down. "But is he, you know, fulfilling all your needs?" Jessica inquired with a smirk on her face.

"Excuse me?" I shot back. OK, time out here, this bitch is hitting on me like a damn man. And seeing that I'm used to being the aggressor, so this was really trippin' me out. "You know what, Jessica, even if he wasn't, I really don't think you could do anything that would make me run to the mountain top and scream out your name."

"Is that right?"

"Ah, yeah."

"Well," Jessica said, "never say never."

"Is that right?" I said.

Jessica just gave me a small smirk as she raised her left eyebrow.

"Well, I hate to say it but if I get with any woman, it will definitely include my man and sorry to say, you aren't quite his cup of," I motioned with my coffee, "well, java."

"No worries beautiful, my feelings aren't hurt because your man isn't interested in my 'java,' as you put it. What I'm interested in is what you have in your java."

I had to laugh at Jessica's play on my words, and as I looked down then back up our eyes locked. I couldn't lie; there was something there, but I wasn't trying to explore it.

"Something funny, beautiful?" Jessica asked as she stepped a few feet closer, running her two fingers discretely across the front of my black, form-fitted DKNY slacks, grazing my vagina ever so slightly. I felt a small tingle. I stepped back.

"Are you always this aggressive?" I said as I took two steps back from her.

"Only with things I want, that act like I can't have 'em."

I'll be damned, I thought, I think I met my damn match. This bitch is me, just not as fine.

"Well, Jessica," I said, "As flattering and disturbing as this is, I have to go. I have a very busy schedule and while I hate to sound like a broken record, I have a man."

"OK, I hear you, but please, just take my card. If anything, maybe we can just be friends," Jessica said and she attempted to extend her card to me for the third time. We locked eyes for a minute.

I reached out, took it and slid it into my pants pocket. She smiled.

"You have a good day, Alana," Jessica said as she turned to leave.

"Yeah, you too," I said as I watched Jessica walk off, jump in her white Range Rover and drive away. There was something about her that I hated, but there was also something about her that I liked.

CHAPTER 7
TODD

I had decided to work from home that day. Sometimes the office can be very distracting and I needed to get through a massive amount of paper work. I logged onto my e-mail account to answer a zillion old e-mails. I told myself that I had to get better at responding more quickly. Usually I would have my assistant answer them, but she would just ask me what to say, so I figured I might as well just do it myself.

I had over one hundred and fifty e-mails waiting for me with about one hundred of those being urgent. As I worked my way down the list, I noticed an email

with an unfamiliar return address. It was an invitation
to Facebook, from a childhood friend in DC whom I
had not seen since grammar school. I had heard about
Facebook but never really paid it much attention. It
just seemed like just a smaller, less convoluted
version of MySpace. I clicked to read the email as
Alana stuck her head in my office.

"Hey baby, you hungry? I made some
sandwiches," she said as she stood in my doorway
with a green and yellow floral waist apron tied around
her small hips.

"Yeah, sure," I said, still preoccupied with the e-
mail.

"I can bring them in here if you can't tear yourself
away from your computer," Alana said, no doubt
gathering that I was pretty engrossed with whatever I
was doing.

"Hey, have you ever heard of Facebook?" I asked,
looking up at her.

"Yeah, it's getting pretty popular. You could find
friends on there that you haven't seen or talked to in
like 20 years, it's pretty amazing."

"So funny, because a childhood friend just sent
me an email to join. Crazy. How do you sign up?" I
asked eagerly, perhaps a little too eager.

"It's easy, let me show you," Alana said as she
walked around to my side of the desk and clicked on
the link that was provided in the email. Alana showed

me in ten minutes how to set up an account, select a password, update my profile and start requesting friends. She even schooled me on how to add photos.

"There ya go," she said, "you are all set up, now you just have start sending out friend requests."

"Thanks baby," I said as I wondered how she knew this and I didn't. "How did you know how to do this? Do you have an account?"

"I do, but I rarely use it. Here, you can send me a request to be friends," Alana said as she typed her name in the Search field. Her picture popped right up.

"Nice picture," I said, admiring one of the many sexy headshots she used as her profile picture. I wasn't sure if I was OK with that.

"That's a pretty sexy shot you have up for your profile picture." I said.

"Baby, I'm a sexy woman - your sexy woman," Alana said as she planted a soft, sensual kiss on my lips. "And don't you forget that."

"How could I?" I said in a playful tone.

"OK, I'm gonna go finish up the sandwiches and bring you one."

"Thanks," I said, directing my attention back to my new Facebook account, knowing I should be working.

Ten minutes later I had successfully shot out 10 friend requests and was browsing through a friend's page when I saw Kai there. The first thing I wondered

was how my friend from DC knew Kai. I
contemplated sending her a friend request, but I
wasn't sure if that was such a good idea, but I
immediately dismissed the thought wondering what
the harm could be? The worst that could happen is
that she won't respond. I clicked the box titled "Add
friend" and sat there as if she would respond
immediately.

Alana walked back in and I quickly minimized the
Facebook window and pulled up my email account.
No need for Alana to know that I was thinking about
Kai. It would be nice to hear from her though, I
thought.

CHAPTER 8
KAI

Two days and two nights passed and each day was just like the next. I lay in the coziness of my couch, wishing for rain on those sunny days. Of course, I had only been in New York for about a week so I was sure my fair share of rain was coming and I shouldn't complain. I was addicted to reality TV, with my latest favorite being The Real Housewives of Atlanta. These damn women were something else, both at the same time entertaining and downright a mess, but I could not turn it off.

I reached for my phone to check my email since I had yet to set up my office, which included my computer, printer and fax. I decided to browse through my Facebook page and saw a request from Todd. My first reaction was to ignore his request, but the idea of knowing what was going on in his life, via Facebook, got the best of me, so I hit "Accept." My phone quickly switched to an incoming call and I noticed it was Simone.

"Hey girl, what up?" I said as I lay back into my pillows on the couch.

"Just checking up on you and the little one. How are you feeling?"

"Pretty good, just relaxing before I have to start work on Monday."

It was weird being in New York while Simone was in Chicago. Especially since I was pregnant, this was the time that I really needed her. I had to keep reminding myself that I chose peace of mind in not running into Todd and Alana. But the question of whether or not I was just running away popped into my head once again.

"I think you're really going like this company," Simone said, "it's so much more laid back than McKenzie and Strong. It will be good for you, especially in your pregger condition."

"Good, I don't need any more added stress in my life right now."

"Have you heard from Todd?" Simone asked hesitantly.

"Funny you should ask that because I just checked my Facebook account and he requested me as a friend. Can you believe that?"

"Of course I can," Simone replied, "he's a man and men don't think twice about adding an ex into the mix, when they're living with a current girlfriend. They're so stupid like that, it's truly amazing how they get through the day. Did you accept his request?"

"I did."

"Really? I would have told him to get over it, he had his shot and he picked the ho."

"Well," I replied slowly, "I am pregnant with his child."

"Yeah, well, technicalities I guess." Simone continued, "Oh, not that you care, but I heard Alana has branched off into acting. Hell, I guess if LisaRaye can do it, anyone with fake tits and a smile has a shot."

I laughed at Simone's comparison, but it was pretty dead on. Alana acting, that can't be much of a stretch since she is so freaking dramatic.

I heard a faint knock at my door and I had a feeling it was probably Toni since I didn't know anyone else in Brooklyn or New York for that matter.

"Hey, Simone, I think the woman who owns the building is knocking on my door, so let me call you back a little later."

"OK honey," she said. "You take care of yourself and I miss the hell out of you."

"I miss you too!"

I slid off the couch and threw on my plush pink robe and matching slippers. The hardwood floors were nice but cold to the touch with my bare feet, so I kept a few pairs of slippers scattered around the house. I saw Toni's reflection in the foyer before clicking on the light and unlocking the door.

"Did I wake you?" Toni asked.

Seeing that it was 5pm in the evening, the question wasn't too farfetched.

"No, no, I was actually watching a Real Housewives of Atlanta marathon ," I said as Toni stepped in, closing the door behind her.

"Ooh, chil', that show is like a train wreck. I can't turn away."

"I know!" I agreed enthusiastically, finding my first thing in common with my new friend.

Toni came in and sat on the loveseat across from the couch, while I quickly put my latest addiction on pause, she made herself comfy.

"So how are you doing? I see you are settling in well."

"Yeah, I am," I said. "I don't start work until Monday so I have a few more days to do nothing."

"Right on. Well, what are you doing this evening, or is this the highlight of it now?" Toni asked, referring to my television and the big dent in my couch that I had successfully made in the last few days since arriving in New York.

"Yep, this is pretty much it," I confessed. "Unfortunately."

"Well, we can't have that. A friend of mine is having a little gathering at her brownstone a few blocks down and I was wondering if you wanted to come with?" Toni asked with a smile.

"As you can see, I haven't really gotten dressed yet," I replied, "and I don't want you to have to wait for me."

"No worries, believe me, I don't mind waiting at all," Toni said with a smile. "Besides, I probably won't be heading down there for a few hours." She shifted on the love seat, trying to get a bit more comfortable.

"Oh, well then," I said, "in that case I guess I could maybe join you. It wouldn't hurt to start making a few friends here in New York, not that you aren't a great first addition."

"Well, I appreciate that," Toni said. "You aren't too bad yourself."

Toni and I shared a smile. I wondered if this was the right time to let Toni know I was pregnant. Although seeing that she was the owner and my landlord, I also wondered if I should have told her before I moved in. Some landlords are weird about tenants having babies.

"So I can come back down and scoop you up at about seven?"

"Yeah, that works," I said. "Um, I guess I should let you in on a little secret."

"Secret?" Toni said as she raised an eyebrow. "What's that?"

"I'm, um, I'm three months pregnant."

Toni sat straight up on the loveseat. "Wow, congratulations! That is just wonderful!" Toni exclaimed with a huge inviting smile on her face. "Girl, you don't look pregnant at all!"

"Yeah, but I'm sure that will change in a few months."

"Of course it will, that's the beauty of pregnancy," Toni said.

"So," I continue, "you're not mad?"

"Mad? Why would I be mad? This is wonderful news," she said.

"Well, I didn't know how you felt about having kids in your place."

"Chil', please! Dogs I mind, but a baby, not at all. I love babies. This is such a blessing. I was just saying to one of my girlfriends the other day how I wish just one of my friends would have a baby, because I love, love babies. I am so happy for you, Kai, really!"

Hearing the joy in Toni's voice made me feel all warm inside. I had been feeling so lonely since moving to New York, and was questioning my move while pregnant and being away from friends and family in Chicago. Toni and I talked for another 20 minutes or so before she headed back upstairs to get ready for the party.

The one great thing I noticed about Toni was that she respected boundaries. Not once did she ask about the baby's daddy, although I got the feeling it wasn't an issue for her.

I turned off my "addiction TV," jumped off the couch and headed for the showers, excited to be heading out that night for a little fun and social interaction. Honestly, it was about time.

Chapter 9
TODD

I think I found my new addiction: Facebook. In the last week I had reconnected with over 50 friends, ranging from grammar school to high school and college. Whoever came up with Facebook was a damn genius. My initial thought when logging on was to see if Kai had accepted my request to be friends, and I noticed that she did. I guessed that was a good thing, although it would have been no big deal if she hadn't accepted. I sat there wondering if I should just leave it at that, with a request. I thought it would be nice to see how she was doing. Would one friendly email hurt? I mean, she's in New York and I'm sure she doesn't have many friends. I quickly opened a message box on Kai's page and typed in how are you? It took a few minutes before I actually hit the send button.

It felt good, I really did miss her a bit, although it wasn't like I was trying to get back with her. There was nothing wrong with being Facebook friends, right?

Alana stuck her head in my office, which startled me. I closed my laptop before she had a chance to see what I was doing. I don't know why I did that, since it's not like I was doing anything wrong, like I said, I leave the drama in the courtroom.

"Hey." I said as I stood and stretched.

"I didn't even know you were home," Alana said as she pulled off her jacket and laid her purse on my desk.

"Yeah, I um, I decided to work from home again this afternoon. I have three briefs to file by next week and didn't want to be disturbed," I said, trying to look extra busy as I shuffled through a few miscellaneous papers on my desk.

"Well, baby, I'm glad to see your practice is really doing great."

"Well," I said, "so long as there is lying, cheating and deceit in marriages, I will be gainfully employed."

"Very true."

"So what are you doing home?" I asked her. "I thought you had a meeting with that movie director about a role." I stood and walked around my desk to give Alana a kiss on the lips.

"I did, but he pushed the meeting until next week, scheduling issues or something. Well, anyway, that's what my agent told me."

"Look at you, Miss Big Shot, with an agent and all. Do I have to have my people call your people?" I asked as I wrapped my arms around Alana's waist, pulling her close to me.

"Maybe," she said. "It depends on how important you are."

"Oh, I'm very important."

"Hmm, I'll be the judge of that counselor."

"Is that so?" I asked as I planted a kiss on Alana's soft lips before making my way back to my office chair and flopping down. "Hey, you want to run to the office with me for a second? I forgot some paperwork I need."

"No, I'm going to take a bath and relax," Alana said. "I'm feeling kind of stressed and I think I need to take it easy."

"Well, the life of a Victoria's Secret model-slash-actress isn't easy, huh?" I asked. "Just make sure you don't forget about me."

"That will never happen as long as you're good," Alana said.

"OK, well, I will be back in 20 minutes. You need anything while I'm out?"

"Why don't you bring back dinner from Edward's?" Alana suggested.

"Sounds like a plan," I said. I grabbed my suit jacket, gave Alana one more kiss and headed out the door.

***

I waited until I heard Todd leave out the front door and drive off before I jumped into Inspector Gadget mode. His ass was up to something when I walked into his office and I was not one to sit back and do nothing about it, that's not my style. I slid behind his desk and sat down.

Todd was notorious for never logging off his accounts, so when I opened up his laptop and I was able to see that he had been browsing through Facebook. Not a huge surprise, since he acted like that damn Facebook was the Second Coming last night. I continued to peruse his page when I noticed he was now friends with Kai Edwards. Huh?

Well, I'll be damned, I thought, that mo-fo has connected with Kai on Facebook. My body temperature immediately started to rise and I wanted to send that little bitch a message from Todd's page and say, "Oh, my bad, fuck off!" Of course, I would never write anything like that, especially since Todd would know that I had been snooping on his account.

Snooping or no snooping, I needed to put a quick stop to that damn reunion. I closed Todd's laptop and immediately started thinking of a game plan. I worked too damn hard to make Todd mine and the last thing I was going to let happen was for Kai to step back into our lives and ruin everything. That just was not gonna fucking happen.

Chapter 10
KAI

Toni and I arrived at a beautiful single-family brownstone on Carleton Ave. She was right – the party was literally a block away. Her friends that owned the home were both attorneys like her, although Toni had transitioned to law professor at NYU, which I think, by the little that I knew of her, suited her much better.

We entered the house and were greeted by the hosts, Kami and Robert Hopper. Kami was a very beautiful woman who was mixed with Asian and

African American parentage. Kami had a very elegant look about her and her personality was infectious. She greeted us with a welcoming smile as Toni introduced me to her and her husband Robert. Robert was a studious looking man with a brown, yellow and white argyle sweater and khaki pants, and his cocoa-colored skin was flawless. They made an adorable couple and for a minute I was more than a bit envious. I wondered in the past when people met Todd and me if they looked at us and admired how we looked together, as well as the life we shared. I've learned from my own life, though, that all that glitters isn't gold.

Toni and I made our way through the small gathering and she introduced me to several people along the way. Everyone was so nice and warm, and I was glad that I had peeled myself off the couch to take Toni up on her offer.

As Toni strayed away to talk to her friends, I made my way through the guests with a polite smile here and there until I found myself standing in the kitchen. I decided to pour myself a glass of Perrier water when I noticed a guy staring at me from the doorway.

He was an interesting looking man and sported a short twist and copper horn-rimmed glasses. His skin was beautiful and looked as if he had just stepped off a plane from some exotic and tropical location. I smiled at him and he quickly smiled back as he began making his way towards me in the kitchen. I looked behind me just to make sure it was me he was aiming for, and since there was no one else standing there, it was clear that I was definitely his target.

"I'm Patrick," he said as he stood in front of me with his hand extended my way.

"Kai. I'm Kai," I said, a bit on the nervous side. I hadn't really expected to meet anyone that night, but then again I was at a party.

"So, how do you know Kami and Robert?"

"Oh, I don't, I just saw some interesting people while walking to the store and decided to stop in," I said, surprised that my humor was still intact.

"Ah, a party crasher, I like that. I hear there's an engagement party going on over on Adelphi Street, so maybe you can hit that before the night is up."

"Sounds like a plan," I said as Patrick smiled back at me then took a healthy sip of his red wine. "Of course I'm kidding," I added.

"Oh, I'm not," Patrick continued. "Can you imagine the food and alcohol we can score?"

I smiled at Patrick's cute personality. "I bet," I said.

Patrick glanced down at my glass of Perrier. "So can I get you something other than water?"

"Oh, no, I'm good, this is strong enough for me right now."

"Are you not a drinker?"

"No I am," I said, "but I'm trying to give my body a bit of a rest."

"Well, good for you," said Patrick. "I need to try that once in a while, but red wine is my downfall."

Toni walked up with a smile.

"Are you bothering my new friend?" Toni said, directing her question to Patrick.

"Of course, but I hope you know that your friend is a party crasher," Patrick said as he gave me a wink.

"Is that right? Well, if she is a crasher then I'm the accomplice." They laughed together as two old friends sharing a moment.

"So how do you two know each other?" I asked, curious about Toni and Patrick's relationship.

"Toni here tortures me every Monday, Wednesday and Friday!" he said.

"Huh?" I responded, not following his train of thought.

"She's my law professor at NYU."

"Ah, right, very cool," I said.

"I think so, although my students have their own opinions," Toni said. "So are you having a good time?"

"I am." I shot back quickly.

"Especially since she met me," Patrick chimed in.

"Easy tiger, Kai is new to the city so you're not allowed to scare her off yet," Toni said, shooting me a smile.

"No, I'm good, Patrick here has been a perfect gentleman – so far," I said with a smirk.

"How do you two know each other if you're new to the city?" Patrick asked me.

"I'm renting the first floor apartment in Toni's building."

"Ah, so you live in the neighborhood," Patrick said.

"You're quick!"

"I try," Patrick shot back as we all had a nice chuckle.

Patrick continued to stare at me, which at that moment started making me feel a bit uncomfortable.

"You look very familiar to me. Where are you originally from?" Patrick asked.

"Chicago, on the north side."

"Ah, I see," Patrick smiled then taking a sip of his red wine. "Maybe you just look like someone I know," Patrick continued.

"I get that a lot," I said.

"Well, it was great meeting you," he said. "I see a fellow classmate I need to go harass. Will you lovely ladies excuse me?"

"Of course," Toni said.

With that Patrick smiled and walked off.

"He seems, uh, interesting," I said.

"Yeah, Patrick is a nice guy," Toni said. "I don't really know him on a social level since he is a student, but I can say this, he is a very intelligent brother."

"Well, that's good to know, but I'm not trying to meet anyone in my current situation," I said.

"Sure, I understand, but friends are always good to have," Toni said.

"This is true."

The more I talked to Toni the more I liked her. She was so warm and comforting and it made me glad our paths had crossed.

"Actually, now that I think about it, I think Patrick might be from Chicago," Toni said as she refilled her glass.

"Really? I wonder why he didn't mention that when he found out I was from there."

"I'm sure it's nothing," Toni said as she took a few sips from her glass.

The night progressed and I met some very interesting people. I never exchanged any more words with Patrick, just a few quick glances, but that was just fine with me. I wanted to leave the party before Toni did because I was getting pretty sleepy, so I walked home after convincing her I would be fine on my short journey back to the brownstone.

I still missed Chicago, although Brooklyn was definitely starting to grow on me.

I climbed into bed and was asleep in minutes, although not before checking my Facebook account to see that Todd had sent me a message – How are you?

I smiled and quickly typed back; Life is good, thanks for asking. I signed off and quickly fell into dreamland.

CHAPTER 11
ALANA

I decided to surprise Todd at work and take him to lunch. No better way to get information out of a person than over white wine and lobster tails. This whole Facebook thing with Todd was really bugging the shit out of me and I was determined to get to the bottom of it.

"Hey, baby," I said as I poked my head into Todd's office, "you busy?"

"Hey, what are you doing here?" Todd asked as he continued to type on his computer. After a moment he stopped to get up and greet me. "This is a pleasant surprise."

"Well, I thought I would come down and take you out to lunch," I said as we embraced. Todd was wearing my favorite cologne and it kind of made me horny.

"I have a court date in a few hours, and I wanted to tie up a few last minute details."

"Well, you can't win cases on an empty stomach," I said, pleading my case.

"What did you have in mind?" Todd asked as he grabbed a few sheets of papers, organizing them before slipping them into his briefcase.

I glanced at my watch. Clearly the wine and lobster were out of the question. But the corner market was definitely an option.

"How about Pete's Café. You love that place and it won't take forever."

Todd took a glance at his watch. "Yeah, that could work."

"Great. My treat, of course," I said with a smile.

"Is that right? Did someone book another movie?"

"Kind of, but I definitely didn't come up here to talk about that," I said, still a bit salty about being offered a role to play a mother to a 22-year-old.

***

We got to Pete's right before the lunch rush and were seated at a table looking out on Michigan

Avenue. Todd was quiet and I knew why. He was mentally preparing for his trial in a few hours.

"So baby, are you ready for this afternoon?" I asked, trying to incorporate some small talk before I hit him with my main agenda.

"Yeah, about as ready as I'm going to be," Todd replied. "This one shouldn't be too hard, though. I'm up against a relatively new lawyer from this firm Anderson and Thomas, so I'm hoping her inexperience will work to my advantage." He took a bite of his roast beef on rye. I realized I only had an hour to do my own cross-examination.

"So, what else is new, baby?" I asked, hoping this would trigger his new love for Facebook.

"Nothing really, just busy as hell at work. But I am definitely not complaining."

"I'm sure. Hey, have you found any more long lost friends on Facebook lately?" I asked, looking up to make eye contact with him.

Todd looked up as if trying to remember something. "Yeah, a few, mainly like high school and college friends. Not too many grammar school friends. Then again, I can hardly remember anyone I went to grammar school with."

"Yeah, tell me about it," I said, thinking he wasn't going to crack. Think Alana, think!

Then I had an idea. "Well, actually, what I've been getting a lot of on Facebook is old flames trying to reconnect. Crazy, huh? I mean, I have in my profile that I am in a relationship, but some people just don't care."

"Well," Todd replied, "are you letting them know that you are off the market?"

"Of course," I said. Clearly you aren't doing the same, I wanted to add;

"That's what I like to hear," Todd said with a smile and a wink.

"Well, what about you, baby?"

"What about me?" Todd repeated as he took another bite of his sandwich.

"I'm sure you have some old flames contacting you, right?"

Todd looked up then back down at his sandwich. "A few, but no one of importance or that you would know."

I just stared at Todd for a moment, not believing what just slipped out from between his lips. "Is that right?" I said as I sucked my damn teeth. Why can't he just come out and say, Yes baby, Kai and I have been communicating, and quite often, I should add. But I saw that Todd was taking the damn fifth.

We continued to eat, but I was pretty much out of conversation at that point. Anger had swooped in and stolen any pleasantries I may have wanted to share. Like my damn daddy used to say, 'If you can't say anything nice, shut the fuck up!'

CHAPTER 12
KAI

It was a beautiful Sunday afternoon and I decided that, instead of staying in and watching reality show after reality show, I would venture out the house and wander around my new neighborhood. The sun was shining on my tree-lined street, making the temperature feel much cooler than the 85 degrees it really was. I walked a few blocks, passing café's and small storefronts until I found myself standing in front of a quaint little bookstore. I headed in to take a closer look. The bookstore was slightly bigger than it looked from the outside and had that wonderful old book smell. I loved that smell. It made me feel good, as if I could sit in there for hours and just read.

The owner of the store was an elderly gentleman with dreads that stretched down to the middle of his back. His face looked as if it could tell stories that should be in history books. I walked up to the regal looking man as he took books from an old rickety cart and placed them on a shelf near the back of the store.

"Hello," I said.

He turned slowly, and with a calm look on his face, replied, "Good afternoon, Queen, and how may I be of service to you?"

"Yes, I was just admiring your bookstore. How long have you had it?"

"Too long to remember," He said, "but it's one of the few left here in Fort Green."

"Oh, wow, that's good to know," I said with a smile on my face, as I looked around the small store.

"Anything special you're looking for?"

"Oh, not really, but I'm always open to something new to read."

"Well, take a stroll," he suggested. "I have just about everything. Have you read Barrack Obama's biography? He was a visitor here, you know. Shocked the living Jesus out of me when he walked through my doors, about a year ago. And now look at him, first black president of the United States. I never thought I would see the day."

I smiled as I watched this small book owner turn into a little chatty Kathy. Initially he had appeared to be a man of few words, but that's what wrong first impressions will do for you I guess.

"Well, thank you for that recommendation, I may just pick it up," I said with a smile. "I'm Kai, by the way. I just moved here from Chicago"

"Well, welcome to New York, Kai, you can call me Jeremiah. You just let me know if you need anything, and I will be right over here."

"Thank you, Jeremiah, I will do that," I said as I turned to browse the bookstore a bit more. I walked toward the front of the store to see Barack's book, and thought, I really should read that. As I picked up the biography and began flipping through its pages, I heard the front door open with a loud squeak. I looked up to see Patrick entering. We immediately made eye contact since the store wasn't bigger than my living room and I was the only patron in the whole place.

He smiled, and I returned his pleasant gesture, thinking what a coincidence it was running into him.

"Well, hello there, Kai," Patrick said as he walked over to me and gave me a friendly hug.

I was a bit taken aback by the overly friendly gesture, since the night I met him he had vanished after talking to me for just a few minutes.

"Hey, how are you, Patrick?"

"I am blessed on this amazingly beautiful day." Patrick looked down at the book that I was holding in my hands. "Ah, Barack Obama's story. Have you read it? Great, great book."

"Ah, no, I actually have not."

"I was looking for you toward the end of the party," he said." I wanted to see if you were interested in grabbing a cup of coffee but Toni told me you already left."

"Yeah, I was kinda tired."

"Well," Patrick asked, "how about now? You interested in grabbing some coffee?"

"Ah, sure," I replied.

"Great," Patrick said as he smiled at me. I wasn't sure how to read him, but I figured it was a bit too early to try to figure him out.

I said my goodbyes to Jeremiah, telling him that I would definitely be back.

Patrick and I headed out of the bookstore and walked a few blocks until we settled in at an inside/outside café. We grabbed a table outside and sat with our lattes, mine being decaf.

"Toni mentioned that you are originally from Chicago," I said, wanting to get that off my chest. I didn't know why but it had been bothering me that he hadn't said anything about it at the party. One thing about Chicagoans is that they are not shy to tell you they are from the great Windy City. Pride in our city is something we learn at a very young age.

"Yes, I am," Patrick said very nonchalantly.

"Interesting," I said.

"I'm sorry?" Patrick said, looking at me with a quizzical look.

"Just that you didn't mention that you were from Chicago when I told you I had just moved from there."

"Oh, right," Patrick said. "Well, I never really mention it since I moved to Brooklyn when I was like 14 so I don't necessarily see Chicago as my home. It's just not a big thing for me. Clearly it is for you."

"Yeah," I said. "I mean, since I did grow up there and all."

"Of course."

"Where did you live in Chicago?" I asked, still trying to get some Chicago facts out of this new friend.

"On the south side, actually."

"Really, whereabouts?" I continued.

Patrick took a sip of his latte then slowly put it back down. "I, um, I can't remember, really. It's been so long."

I smiled, although my gut feeling was telling me that he knew. He just didn't want to say.

"I see. Well, I take it you love Brooklyn since you've been here for a while."

"No doubt, Brooklyn is definitely my home. I plan on raising my family here," Patrick said with a note of enthusiasm and pride in his voice.

"I could see raising a family here, too," I said as I took a sip of my coffee.

"What about you Kai? Do you see yourself having a family?"

Patrick's question threw me, and I felt my stomach tighten. I wondered if Toni tipped Patrick off that I was pregnant. Then I thought, I really don't think Toni is that type of person.

"Well, I'm not sure. I'm just trying to see if New York is a good fit for me right now."

"Oh, so you may jump ship and move back to the Midwest?"

"It all depends on my circumstances," I said hesitantly.

"Like what?"

"Well," I said, "if I actually like New York enough to make it my permanent home, and a few other factors."

"Factors like…?"

Patrick was trying to turn the tables on me and get personal with the questions. But these were not questions I was ready to answer; especially to someone I'd just met a few days earlier.

"Just things that I really don't want to discuss right now," I said in the most polite voice I could muster up.

There was an awkward moment and I felt it was time to end this intimate get together. I glanced at my watch to add a bit of urgency to my next statement. "Well, I actually have to get going, I start work tomorrow and I have a few things I have to take care of," I said, wondering if he were going to ask me, "Like what?"

"Oh, of course," Patrick said, standing as I got up to grab my purse. "Well, thank you for having a cup of coffee with me."

"Oh, sure, no problem," I said.

"Maybe we can do it again soon."

"Sure," I said, thinking to myself, Maybe not.

As I left the café I glanced back to see Patrick sitting down to finish his coffee. Patrick was a nice guy but there was something about him that gave me a weird feeling inside.

Chapter 13
KAI

"How is work?" my Therapist asked as she gave me a warm smile.

"It's good. I'm just trying to get settled in and get to know New York a little better, but, so far I think I'm gonna like working there," I said, as I laid on my left side on Dr. Albright's leather chaise lounge.

"Good, I'm glad to hear that, and I take it you're settling in to your new home here in Brooklyn, as well?"

"Yeah, as much as to be expected I guess. But only time will tell," I said.

"Of course," Dr. Albright said as she took a deep breath and crossed her right leg over her left. She was wearing a pair of Jimmy Choo black pumps, which kind of took me by surprise since I would have never thought of her as a designer footwear woman. She seemed much more of a Payless type.

"Nice shoes," I said, wondering if it was appropriate to compliment your therapist on her shoes.

"Thank you," she said, "They were actually a gift from my sister."

Aha, that explains it, I thought, although they did look good on her. I wanted to tell her that she should let her sister shop for her shoes more often, but I knew that would be inappropriate on any level.

"Kai, I want to talk to you today about Todd."

"I really wanted to talk about this new guy I met," I said, "maybe see if you can figure out what is different about him."

"OK, well, we can talk about the new guy a little later," Dr. Albright said, "but I think we should really start addressing some of the issues related to Todd."

It was my turn to take a deep breath as I shifted my body a bit and lay flat on my back, staring up at the ceiling.

"I guess I should tell you that he reached out to me on Facebook."

"Facebook? That's sort of a networking website, right?" Dr. Albright asked.

"I don't know how much networking is done," I answered, "but it is definitely a way to stay in touch with people, as well as delve into their personal lives."

"So he sent you an e-mail?"

"Yeah, sort of, it was more like a short message. Nothing deep or anything, just to say hello."

"And how did you feel about that?"

"Surprised," I said, "but not shocked."

"Why is that?"

"Because Todd is a 'buyer's remorse' type of guy. You know the people who buy something and then are ready to return it the next day? That's Todd. He's probably having this internal battle over what he did."

"As far as?"

"Deciding to be with Alana over me," I said, finishing her sentence. "I know him. But the difference with Todd is that he will keep something even though he knows he should return it."

"Why do you think he does that?" she asked.

"Because he lacks balls, Dr. Albright, that's why," I said, feeling that sense of resentment fill my body.

Dr. Albright looked down at her yellow pad and scribbled a few lines, then looked back up at me, appearing unaffected by my previous comment. "So did you respond to his message?"

"I did. I mean, he is the father of my unborn child," I explained, "and eventually he will find out and will need to help me financially."

"Is that all you want from him, financial help?"

"No. I would also like him to choke on his own vomit and die," I added, "but then my child would be fatherless and that wouldn't be good."

Dr. Albright grimaced as she uncrossed her legs and wrote a bit more in her yellow pad. I wondered if my off-color comments had annoyed her or if she just rolls with the punches. In her line of work, I'm sure she hears and secs much, much more.

"Do you feel you and Todd had a healthy relationship?" Dr. Albright asked as she stopped writing and looked at me.

"Yeah, for the most part. I guess it was me who changed it all when I started, you know, sleeping with Alana, his best friend. Although he did have a baby with her which he never revealed, so in hindsight he was just as at fault in screwing up the relationship."

"OK. Now I want to transition over to Alana for a minute," Dr. Albright said.

Just the mere mention of Alana's name created tension in my body, and although I didn't want to talk about her, I stepped right into it. This woman was good.

"I realize you have a lot of resentment towards Alana and that is understandable, but repressing those feelings only hurts you in the end."

Dr. Albright had a good point, but I still wasn't ready to give up those ill will feelings. Not yet anyway. So I remained silent and let Dr. Albright talk.

"Were you in love with her?" she asked.

Whoa. That was a question I wasn't prepared for. I thought for a second, Should I come clean? I was here to be honest, not be judged.

I shifted in my seat. "I don't know. I don't think so, I think it was more infatuation and the fact I'd never been with a woman."

"And how did you like that," the doctor asked, "being with a woman for the first time?"

"It was different. Fun."

"And how did you feel when it came to Todd, when you were sleeping with Alana?"

"I felt guilty as hell," I said, "but I couldn't stop."

"Why do you think you couldn't stop?" she persisted.

I thought about Dr. Albright's question for a minute before responding. It was a hard question, one I constantly asked myself during the affair. "I don't know. I think she had this control over me, this, this power."

Dr. Albright put her pad down in her lap and looked over at me. "One thing I learned in life Kai, is that no one can control how you feel, how you act or what you do. There is something within us that relinquishes that control to them."

"Really?' I asked.

"Yes," Dr. Albright said as she slowly nodded her head. She picked her pad up again and wrote a few lines.

"Kai, your relationship with Todd was not 100% healthy because you were lacking something, and it was that something that made you stray to Alana."

I slowly lifted my head up from the chaise, as something kind of clicked with Dr. Albright's last statement. "OK, what was it?"

Dr. Albright smiled at me with that warm smile. "That's something you have to figure out on your own," she said and glanced at her watch. I knew our time was nearly over, but I wasn't ready for it to end. I felt like I had just "got" something. I sat up on the chaise and took a swig of my water that had been sitting on the table to my right. I realized that we never got to the subject of Patrick, though maybe that was a good thing. Maybe I was overreacting about how he came across. Besides, I needed to stay focused on why I was in therapy in the first place.

"Thank you, Dr. Albright," I said as I stood and headed out of her office, but not before hearing her reply.

"Kai, work on releasing the guilt you feel for cheating on Todd. That's where you will start finding your answer."

Dr. Albright's last comment resonated with me as I slowly walked home, feeling as if I were floating rather than taking steps. I knew I had never let go of the guilt and shame I felt for cheating on Todd. I knew it was time to do just that.

Chapter 14

ALANA

We were between shoots on my new indie film
and I needed some alone time. I couldn't get the
conversation I'd had with Todd over lunch out of my
head. How dare his ass deny sending Kai messages on
Facebook? Maybe he isn't 100% over her ass, I
thought, but if that's the case, I will make it my job to
see that he is.

I found a comfy looking chair down the hall near
an empty room, which I assumed they used as a set
and settled in on it. I knew I needed to use this time to

go over my lines, but my mind was too clouded with Todd and Kai. We were shooting in an old warehouse downtown on Randolph Street and in my opinion this place screamed "low fucking budget!" But who was I to judge, seeing this was my first film and all? I was pretty sure Halle Berry had to endure the same conditions in the beginning of her career, so I too, was willing to sacrifice.

I lay my head back and tried to figure out why Todd would lie to me, or for that matter, why he would want to communicate with Kai in the first place. I mean, what was the point? She clearly cheated on him with me, and Todd and I have a child together, something Kai couldn't give him. Just thinking about Kai's infertility issues brought a small feeling of joy to my being. Todd may have toyed with the fact that he missed her and had thoughts of maybe getting back with her, but Todd wanted kids of his own and Kai was all dried up. I think that's what frustrated me so much, why would he even open up lines of communication with her? What was the damn point?

I continued to have an internal conversation with myself when I felt a presence standing over me. I opened my eyes to see my agent, Emanuel, staring down at me.

"There you are. Not answering your cell phone today?" Emanuel asked, a slight edge of attitude in his voice.

I pulled out my phone to see that I had missed seven calls, five of which were from him.

"What's going on?" I asked, looking up at him. Emanuel reminded me of Mr. Jay from "America's Next Top Model." His porcelain mocha Puerto Rican skin would make any woman envious of his genes, especially ones who have to drop hundreds of dollars a months to get what he has naturally. Gay or not, Emanuel was a beautiful man and I knew his nights were rarely spent alone.

"The director just gave me these new pages," Emanuel said as he extended a revised script my way.

"More changes?" I asked with obvious irritation in my voice. "I haven't memorized the old ones yet," I said, grabbing the script and quickly flipping though it.

"Well, I suggest you get on it. What are you doing way over here anyway, being anti-social? You got drama on the personal side, darlin'?

"No. Well, OK, maybe a little."

"OK," Emanuel asked, "what happened?"

"It's Todd," I said, "I think he's trying to get back with his ex."

"Kendall?"

"Kai."

"Right," he replied. "Well, what makes you think that?"

"Because he's been talking to her on Facebook."

"So?"

"So!?!" I fumed.

"Do you know how many people I talk to on Facebook that I wouldn't fuck with someone else's dick? Child, there was this one guy…"

"Ah, hello!" I interrupted. "Can we please focus on me, Miss Thing? Thank you."

"OK, well," he sighed, "what's your point then?"

"My point is," I said slowly, "I confronted Todd about it and he fucking denied it, to my face."

Emanuel stared at me for a second as he shifted his weight from his left foot to his right. "Is that it?"

"What do you mean is that it? He lied to me!"

"Uh huh, and how long did you lie to him about fucking his girlfriend?"

"Wait a minute, I told you that?" I asked, searching my memory database.

"Girlfriend," Emanuel said, "your flappin' has a way of working against you."

"Clearly," I said, realizing that I had revealed way too much personal info to my gay agent, which was hard not to do when he came off like a damn woman. I had to get more girlfriends, I told myself.

I sat back in my comfy chair, thinking that Emanuel had a good damn point, but I was afraid that

I had too much to lose if Todd decided to get back together with Kai.

"Listen, darlin', forget about Todd and Kai, you are with him now and you two have a child together, they don't. And never will. Sweetheart," he continued, "if you continue to obsess you will conveniently obsess your cute little ass right out of this movie, you got it?" Emanuel spoke with a stern and not so gay tone in his voice. All he needed was the two snaps and a circle to drive his point home.

"Fine," I said, "I'm done."

"Thank you," he sighed. "You have your new lines, OK?" Emanuel said, looking down at the script in my hand. "Now do me a favor and learn them. You are back up in 30."

I stared at my new lines as Emanuel turned away, leaving me alone in my comfy chair. I realized that I needed to stay focused. In the back of my mind I knew that Todd and I were bound by the fact that we have a child together, but I kept hoping my secret would never be revealed.

Chapter15
TODD

I had a ton of paperwork to get through and my head was already spinning from my court case earlier that morning. Divorce was a funny thing. One day you are madly in love with each another, and the next, you want to make the other person as miserable as Tom Cruise in a straight marriage. I leaned back in my black leather high-back chair and rubbed my temples. Kai popped into my head and I wondered what would have come of us if we had ever gotten married. Would we have been going through a nasty divorce by now or would we have tried to work it out? I didn't think people took their vows seriously anymore. I mean, it says in black and white to have and to hold, for better for worse, for richer for poorer, in sickness and in health, to love and to cherish, till death us do part.

Till death us do part, now that was a commitment not to be taken lightly. I took a deep breath and felt a sadness come over me. I missed my friendship with Kai, but I guessed there wasn't much I could do about it now, I'd made my decision and I had to honor it.

I focused back on the tremendous amount of paperwork staring at me, knowing it wasn't going to write itself. Not only did I have tax returns to review and credit card bills to dissect, but I also I needed to prepare a list of questions for the witnesses.

I opened my e-mail account and noticed I had a message from Kai. Hmm, I thought, I guess, "I thought her up" as my auntie Frances used to say. I eagerly opened the e-mail to see that she had responded to my previous message. I clicked to reply, which took me straight to my Facebook account. As I waited for the message screen to open, I contemplated how I really should be working this networking site to help expand my business. There has to be a way to incorporate personal addiction with potential income.

I clicked in the message box to respond to Kai's e-mail and began writing eagerly: "So what's new in

New York?" I looked at what I written and for a minute wondered if it was too much, and wondered if she would think I was prying. I actually wanted to write much more, but my gut told me to start small. As my index finger hovered over the mouse button, I thought, 'what am I doing? What are my intentions?' My head was swirling but one thing I knew for sure was that I didn't want to lose contact with Kai. I was just about to hit "Send" when Maceo stuck his head in my office.

"Hey, you busy?" Maceo asked as he stood in the doorway waiting for a response.

"Always. What's going on?" I said, looking up while simultaneously minimizing my Facebook screen.

"Wanted to see if you were free for lunch, wanted to run a few things by you about a case I just got."

"Outside referral?" I asked.

"You could say that," Maceo replied as he made his way into my office. He was wearing a light pink shirt, black pinstriped pants and a shiny black tie. Maceo was one of those few brothers that could wear a pink shirt and get away with it. Or as he liked to tell me, not every brother can rock pink the way I do and look good!

"So what's the backstory on this one?" I asked pulling my work back up on my monitor and trying to make sure I wasn't missing anything.

"Long story short," Maceo began, "I was at this chick's house the other night and her girlfriend called up crying, all hysterical and shit. So when she hung up, I, the sensitive brother that I am, asked her what was wrong."

"Sensitive?" I joked, knowing there was no portion of sensitivity in Maceo, just hustle.

"Well, you know," he went on, "I had to at least act like it!" He smoothed out his shirt and straightened his tie.

"So, get this, her girl has only been married for one year to this rich mofo who didn't sign a pre-nup and on top of that, had an affair with her younger sister who is only 17."

"What?"

"Yeah."

"Damn," I said.

"'Damn' is putting it lightly," Maceo said, "Because he's pretty much fucked. Personally, I think the wife and sister set his dumb ass up, but he's the one who fell for the shit."

"How old is the husband?" I asked.

"I'd say about seventy-five."

"And the wife?"

"Twenty-five."

"Wow," I said, shaking my head.

"Yep, the American dream," Maceo said with a huge smile on his face.

"Sounds like a slam dunk."

"Well, you know how I do," Maceo said as he smoothed out his shirt and adjusting his skinny tie again. "Gonna take Daddy dumb-bucks for all his chips and then some."

I was always amazed at how Maceo found these cases, but as long as it kept Daniels and Smith out of the red, I was not complaining.

"So you good for lunch? It's on me," Maceo said.

"I can't, I'm swamped... but, rain check?"

"Of course. I guess I could call Kimberly; she owes me a quickie. No better way to shake the Monday mid-day blues, right?"

"Hey," I said, "just be back for our afternoon meeting."

"No doubt!" Maceo said as he stood to leave.

"Hey, let me ask you something before you leave, not job-related," I said, catching Maceo just before he disappeared out of my office.

"What's up?" he asked.

"Have you ever contacted an ex when you were in a new relationship?"

Maceo walked back over to my desk, saying, "It depends on how good the sex was."

"The sex?" I asked.

"You know, was she a fire head or if the pussy was on ten."

"OK, even though that sounds great, I'm thinking more along the lines of friendship," I replied slowly.

"Oh, right," Maceo said as he paused to ponder my question. I knew Maceo didn't really relate women to friendship, but I figured I'd take my chances.

"Well, there was this one girl. We actually got busy, in a Porta-Potty no less. Now that was some crazy shit."

"A Porta-Potty?" I said, raising one eyebrow.

"Baby girl wanted to get dirty and we were at the Taste of Chicago, so no better way, right?"

"Let me just lay out where I am going with this question," I continued. "You know that I'm dating Alana now, and that Kai and I are done, right?"

"Right, right."

"But even though Kai and I are history," I said, "we've been exchanging e-mails through Facebook."

"Really? Have you tapped it again?" Maceo asked.

"No, she's in New York."

"New York, that's right. There are some fine ass honey's in New York," Maceo said as he massaged his five o'clock shadow then adjusted his manhood. "Do you want my professional opinion?"

I laughed to myself at how serious Maceo took himself. "Oh, yes, doctor, please, that's why I asked you," I said, realizing I may have to take it with a grain of salt.

Maceo looked up to the ceiling; collecting his thoughts, then back down at me. "If it don't fit, you must acquit"

"What?"

"If it don't fit, you must acquit," Maceo said again with a little more feeling.

"In Maceo terms, please," I said impatiently.

"If you don't get caught, then what's the harm? As my mama used to say, 'don't throw the baby out with the bath water,' which is a motto I use quite often in my dating life."

"I see," I said, nodding.

Although Maceo had a twisted way of viewing dating life, he had a valid point.

"Bottom line, bro," he said, "Alana may be Miss Right now, but you don't know if she is equipped for the long haul until you take her for a test drive, you know, break her in. You said you two have been friends for what, 13 years? But in those 13 years have you ever dated her, woke up next to her, day after day, week after motherfucking week?" Maceo asked and he shook his head. "Now that is where the test comes in, believe me. Been there and definitely done that." Maceo locked eyes with me, and continued. "Don't throw out the baby with the bathwater. Think about it. Maceo has spoken. So, can I bring you back a sandwich or something, maybe a smoothie?"

"No," I answered, "I'm good. Thanks for the advice by the way."

"Anytime. I'm here for you, bro," Maceo said as he left my office.

I glanced down at my computer and pulled my Facebook account back up. My message was still there unsent. I stared at it for a second before clicking 'send'.

Chapter 16
KAI

I really did live for the weekends. It was another beautiful Saturday and I decided to finish doing some of my long overdue unpacking. I opened up all the windows, put on some house music and danced myself around my new abode, unpacking, storing and organizing my new space. It felt good to be in New York, to have a great job and interesting friends.

The music was blaring and I didn't realize my cell phone was ringing until I danced past my dining room table to see the screen lit up. Corrine was calling. My mom had a way of calling at the most inopportune times. I quickly grabbed the remote of my iHome music system and pressed "Pause," hoping I could catch her call before it fell into voicemail.

"Hey, mom," I said, a bit out of breath, realizing that being pregnant took a bit more out of me, even to dance.

"Hello, dear, did I catch you at a bad time? Why are you out of breath, you're not overexerting yourself, are you?"

My mom had a habit of rattling off a series of questions as if you were supposed to keep notes and then answer them all back in order.

"No, mother," I said, "I am cleaning and it is all good, I'm fine. So, how are you?"

"Oh, other than dealing with your father's mood swings and of course, my monthly women's group, life is splendid."

I decided to take a seat while talking to Corrine. Sometimes our conversations could get a bit lengthy. So I headed back to my office where I flopped in front of my computer. I figured I could answer a few e-mails while listening to Corrine talk about her life. As my mom continued to talk about my father, her social group and an annoying pain in her hip, I noticed I had a message from Todd: So what's new in New York?

I clicked on the link and it took me to a response box, so I began to type. I am doing well, New York is, well New York. How are things in Chicago? I tried not to think about Todd being with Alana, but the fact was, they were together and I just had to get over it.

"Honey, are you there?" my mom asked, pulling me back to her world and out of the one that included my past with Todd and Alana.

"Yes, yes, I am. So how is dad?" I asked, hoping we could keep the subject on him for a while.

"He misses you, as do I. I still don't understand why you had to run off to New York, especially when you are carrying my grandchild. Does Todd know yet?"

"I told you mom," I replied, "I just needed a change and, no, Todd doesn't know yet."

"Well, honey, what are you waiting for? He has a right to know."

"I know this mom," I said, feeling the slightest headache begin to permeate my temples. I needed to get my mother off of me and on to something else fast.

"So how is Mila doing with her divorce?" I asked, hoping that would divert my mother's third degree.

"Your twin sister is just fine, I don't think I have seen her this happy since she got her first pair of Kate Spade pumps in high school. But I didn't call to talk about Mila; I need to know when you are coming home. You know you can come home to visit."

"I know mom, but I haven't even been in New York a month yet, give me a little time to settle in."

"I could always come to visit you," she said. "Actually, I could come up next weekend if you like."

I knew my mom was fishing for a visit, and right now I wasn't mentally prepared to spend three days with Corrine, especially without the comfort of alcohol to ease the pain. I definitely had to veto that request.

"Actually, mom, next weekend wouldn't be good."

"Why not sweetheart?"

"Because I have to work," I said, thinking the moment that lie came out of my mouth that I had just opened up a new can of worms.

"Work! Why in God's name do they have you working on the weekends? Do they know you're pregnant?"

"Of course they do, but I decided to work a few extra hours to get myself up to speed. It's no big deal, mom. Really." I said as I cradled the phone between my ear and shoulder so I could massage my temples with my index fingers. I closed my eyes only to open them upon hearing my doorbell ringing. Thank gawd, I thought, saved by the bell. I had no idea who could be ringing my doorbell on a Saturday afternoon, I didn't care. What I did care about was it gave me an excuse to get off the phone. My doorbell rang again for the second time, and this time Corrine actually heard it.

"What is that noise, honey?"

"Oh, mom, shoot, someone's at the door. Let me call you back, I think it's a package I'm expecting."

"Well, I can just hold, sweetheart."

"Actually, it would be better if I called you back; I think this will take longer than a minute."

"Fine," she said, "I know when I'm being pushed off." Oh lord, I thought, now here comes the guilt parade. "You've never made me a priority in your life," she added.

"Mom…"

"Don't worry," she said, "I will be just fine. Give your mother a call when you find the time to talk. I still love you."

"I love you too, mom."

Corrine hung up. Why do I do this to myself? I wondered. Now on top of my mom thinking I ran away from her, I also had to contend with the guilt from a simple freaking phone call.

I tossed my phone onto my desk and headed toward my foyer to see Patrick standing on my porch. My first thought was that I didn't remember telling him where I lived, just that I lived in Brooklyn.

Secondly, I wasn't in the mood for company, especially his company right now.

I opened my door as he stood there, pulling Barack Obama's book from behind his back. "I thought you might need some reading material," he said with a big smile.

I smiled back thinking that it was a nice gesture, him buying this book for me, which turned his unpleasant interruption into a pleasant surprise. "Wow, thank you very much," I said as I reached out to accept my gift. "This was very thoughtful of you. Would you like to come in?"

"If it's not too much of a bother, I would love to," Patrick said as he entered my house, closing the door behind him. "Nice, I like what you've done here," Patrick said, admiring my space.

"Thanks," I said. "By the way, how did you know where I lived?"

"It wasn't hard to figure out after you mentioned at Kami's and Robert's party that you lived in Toni's first floor unit."

"OK, I did say that, huh?"

"Yep," Patrick replied. "Toni actually held a few classes down here when the place was vacant. I hope you don't mind me just stopping by, I was taking a stroll and looked up and here I was, in front of your place."

"And you just so happened to have Obama's book in your hand," I said with a smile.

"OK. All right, so I'm busted. I felt bad about our coffee date the other day and I wanted to come by to apologize."

"For what?" I asked.

"Well, for being a bit evasive as well as intrusive for starters." he said.

"Yeah, you did swing from one side of the pendulum to the other."

"I tend to do that a lot and it can come off as a bit weird. Believe me," he went on, "I'm not as weird as you may be thinking."

"Oh, I don't think you're weird," I said, although I did think he was walking the tightrope.

"Sure you do" he said, "but that's OK."

We both kind of smiled.

"Well, I too want to apologize for being a bit, well, evasive and intrusive, as well."

"Aha, by golly," Patrick exclaimed with a smile, "So we do have something in common."

I was still trying to put my finger on this man, he was definitely very intelligent and on the nerdy side, but I didn't quite get his humor. I guess I should just stop trying and let what ever happens unfold.

"You're funny."

"And you're adorable," Patrick said with a smile.

I felt a bit uncomfortable with that, especially since I knew I must've looked like hell. And I was not at all sure where this relationship was headed. I needed to come clean with him so there wouldn't be any misunderstanding.

"Did you want something to drink?" I asked, changing the subject. I was good at that, an Edwards's family trait.

"Sure, what do you have?"

I realized after offering up a beverage all I had was water. I needed to get to the market. "I actually just have water, sorry."

"No, water is fine," he said. "I love water."

I smiled at Patrick's way of going with the flow. "OK then, one water coming right up," I said as I headed toward the kitchen to get him a glass of water with ice.

Patrick ended up staying for a few hours as we talked about everything, from his family to mine as well as why he decided to become a lawyer. After about two hours I was comfortable enough to reveal to him why I would not want our friendship to be more than a friendship.

"There's something I need to share with you, OK?"

"Wait, don't tell me, you need a kidney and I am your only hope."

I smiled at Patrick's corny humor. It was kind of refreshing, actually.

"Close, but not quite. Sorry to disappoint you, though, I know how much you wanted to give up a body part."

"So, what's up?" he asked.

"Well, I just want to be on the up and up with you. I like you and I would love to be friends with you. With friendship comes honesty."

"Hmm, this sounds serious. You're not dying are you?"

"No," I said. "I am pregnant."

"Are you telling me I'm the father?" Patrick asked in a joking way.

"No, stop being silly."

"OK, sorry, I have officially turned off the silliness."

"On the real," I continued, "I'm three months pregnant and the father of my child is with his best friend."

"The best friend is a female, right?"

"Oh yeah, right," I replied, "I should have been more clear."

"Well you gotta ask, since it is the new millennium and all."

I laughed at Patrick's quip. "Yeah, it is. You can understand my hesitance in being anything more than just a friend."

Patrick looked at me and said, "Listen Kai, I appreciate your honesty, I really do, but I really just want to be your friend, nothing more. I like to think of myself as an insightful sort of guy and to be honest, I felt that friendship vibe the moment we met."

"Really?"

"Yeah. Believe me, I would be honored to just be your friend. And to be honest, you wouldn't be able to handle all of this."

I laughed out loud at Patrick's attempt to be suave.

"What's so funny?" he asked with mock shock. "I'm a catch."

"No, I know you are, I'm just laughing at, well, never mind," I said as Patrick chuckled along with me.

Patrick stayed for a few more hours and we talked and laughed, getting to know each other as the weirdness I felt about him slowly subsided. He left but not without making plans to hang out with me again soon.

Chapter 17
TODD

I walked into my condo to see Alana and Riley
eating dinner. The moment I entered, I knew I should
have waited to eat until I got home. There was only
one thing that smelled so food, take-out from
Edgardo's Pizza.

"Hey," I said. I dropped my briefcase on the
counter and headed over to greet Riley and Alana
with kisses.

"Hey, baby, you hungry?" Alana asked as she swallowed the last bit of food in her mouth as she kissed me back.

Alana wasn't a big cook - she was good at a lot of things but cooking wasn't one of them. But I had to give it to her – she had ten different restaurants on speed dial and knew who would be able to have a meal delivered in minutes. Usually by now, I would be famished since it was almost 8pm, but my assistant had ordered food for the office in anticipation of everyone working late. Fortunately for me, we had wrapped up sooner than expected.

I kissed Riley on the forehead. "Thanks, but I ate dinner at the office."

"Oh," Alana said with a slight disappointment in her voice.

"But save it, I can take some for lunch tomorrow. So how was your day?" I asked.

"Other than fumbling through my lines, I can't complain," Alana said, shrugging her shoulders.

"Is the movie not going well?" I asked.

"It's fine, I just have a lot on my mind," Alana said with a forced smile.

I knew something was bothering Alana, but I didn't know what it could be. I knew Alana though, and there was no doubt it would come out eventually.

"OK," I said and I gave Alana and Riley another kiss before grabbing my briefcase.

"Where are you going?" Alana asked.

"I have to reply to some last-minute e-mails. Don't worry, I won't be working all night, I'm beat." I said as I headed towards my office. Kai's e-mail reply was at the forefront of my mind. I knew what I was doing was risky, but I hated how things had ended with us and, if anything, there may still be a chance we could be friends.

I sat down behind my desk, pulled out my laptop and went directly to my Facebook account without passing 'Go". Four messages were waiting for me and I was happy to see that one of them was from Kai. I clicked on her message and her short reply:I am fine, New York is New York, how is Chicago?

I smiled and hit "Reply." It was only right to send her a message back in return.

I looked up, thinking I heard Alana coming down the hall, but I think that was my guilt playing tricks on me. I typed Kai a quick response: Chicago is pretty good, I can't complain. I hope all is well with you, Kai. I chuckled to myself, not seeing Alana was now standing in the doorway watching me.

"What's so funny?" Alana asked.

"Hey, I didn't hear you come in."

"That must be some e-mail," she said.

I felt a tinge of irritation rising in me, but chose to ignore it. "Yeah, it's from Maceo, and we both know the things that come out of his mouth."

"Oh, really, like what?" Alana gave me a fake half-smile and folded her arms in front of her.

"You know Maceo, just more of his charm and inappropriate stuff." I minimized my Facebook account and pulled up my work e-mail. "So, um, what's up, babe?"

"Riley wants you to read her a bedtime story."

"Oh, wow," I replied, "Can you do it? I wanted get through these e-mails before it gets too late."

"I tried," Alana said, "but she wants you."

I took a deep breath, knowing that it was impossible to say no to your child requesting a simple bedtime story. "OK, I will be up in a second," I said. I turned back to my screen as I read through a few of my work e-mails. Alana turned slowly to leave and headed out of my office. When I looked back up to make sure she was gone I hit "Send" and closed down my laptop before heading out my office.

***

I watched from the kitchen as Todd headed upstairs to read Riley a bedtime story. I hoped Riley wouldn't spill the beans that it was my idea and not hers, but she loved it when Todd read to her so I doubted she will make a big deal about it. I made sure the coast was clear and knew I had to work fast since Todd's bedtime stories were usually faster than the norm.

I put a few dirty plates in the sink before I headed towards Todd's office to sneak a peek at just what he was laughing at. Twenty bucks said it had nothing to do with his ignorant ass colleague, Maceo.

I opened his laptop and sure enough, there it was, his Facebook account, open and ready to be read like a book. Men like him never cover their tracks. That's why they always get caught.

I scanned Todd's Facebook "wall" and saw nothing of interest that made me suspicious. I was pressed for time so I had to work fast. I immediately clicked on his messages and there it was - a brand new message from Kai with a response back from Todd. As I read Todd's message, two words stuck out to me: New York. What was Kai doing in New York? But more importantly, why the hell didn't Todd mention to me that she was living there?

I decided to click on Kai's Facebook page to see if something would confirm that she was indeed in New York – and, sure enough, she was. Strangely, this made me feel a bit better about the whole thing. I glanced at my watch, ten minutes had passed and it was likely that Todd was wrapping up his bedtime story with Riley. I was about to close out his page when I saw a message on Kai's wall that made me take a closer look. It was from a woman named Toni and it read: Had a good time with you the other night, we should go out again soon.

I wondered if Kai were dating women in New York, I mean, just because she slept with me and regretted it didn't mean she was done exploring. I thought to myself, this is good. No, this is better than good. My mind started to churn. A few more minutes passed and I was getting nervous, because if Todd found me on his computer he would flip out. I whipped out my Blackberry and sent him a text: You still reading to Riley? Todd sent one right back: Yes, almost done, she is getting sleepy.

I knew that meant I had at least a few more minutes left to snoop. I clicked on this Toni woman's page and before I could read all her info, I saw a very familiar looking face with a name, Jessica McCoy. Jessica McCoy? I know that name, but from where?

Suddenly, it hit me. Jessica McCoy was the lesbian from the other night who wouldn't stop hitting on me. I thought it was more than just an odd coincidence that she was friends with this Toni woman and Toni knows Kai.

I heard Todd moving upstairs, which meant he was done and on the move. I glanced back down at the screen to read Jessica's message to Toni, which said: Miss you, babe, when will I see your beautiful face again. Come visit me in Chicago, I'm lonely. A smile spread across me face. I knew I had just stumbled on my ace in the hole.

I clicked back to Todd's home page before minimizing his screen and jumping from behind his desk.

"What are you doing in here?" Todd's voice startled me a bit. I expected him back downstairs but not that damn quickly.

"Hey, is Riley asleep?"

"Yeah, she is," Todd said as he made his way back behind his desk.

"Great," I said. By then I was near his bookcase.

"What are you doing in here?" Todd asked again.

"Oh, I was looking for an interesting book to read before I got in bed tonight and thought you would have something I could borrow. You don't mind, do you, baby?"

"Of course not," Todd said as he slowly sat down and opened his computer back up. "But my fiction books are over on the other bookcase, those are all law books."

"Oh, my bad," I said as I chuckled and sashayed over to the bookcase on the opposite side of his office, grabbed the first book that I laid eyes on then turned towards Todd. "You gonna be much longer, baby?"

"Ah, not really, I just have few more e-mails to return," he said as his eyes went back and forth from his laptop to me. I bet you do, I thought to myself.

"OK, well, take your time," I said, thinking to myself, No rush. I had the information I needed to move forward with my plan.

Chapter 18
KAI

"When are you going to tell Todd you're knocked up with his seed?" Simone asked as I chatted with her at work. I had called Simone while still on the speakerphone and I suddenly regretted it as I heard her words echo through my office. "Simone, I'm at work and your ass is on speaker," I said. Hopefully no one in my office heard her latest speaker-gram.

"Damn, bitch, you haven't even told your boss you're pregnant? What the hell are you waiting for? It's not like you're Angelina Jolie and the whole world is waiting with bated breath for you to make an announcement. You're Kai 'who cares' Edwards," Simone said in her joking tone. I loved how Simone kept it real, sometimes too real.

"I will tell my boss in a few weeks," I said, "as far as Todd goes, I'm not sure yet. Sooner rather than later though."

"Ah, yeah, telling him on the child's first birthday wouldn't be great planning on your part."

"Of course not," I replied.

"Hey, when you tell him, can I be on the phone? My life is so goddamn boring these days I could use the entertainment. I swear I gained about 15 pounds listening to stories about you, Alana and Todd. Damn, those were the days. You would call, I would break out the Doritos and Oreos. Although, now that I think about it," she went on, "your life is just as boring as mine these days. One of us needs to spice it up, so come on! Let's call Todd right now on three-way so I can listen. I'll put my phone on mute."

"Ah no."

"Come on, I just ordered lunch and it would be nice to have a little bit of entertainment while I eat."

"No, Simone."

"Why not?" she pleaded. "You're such a killjoy."

"Simone!"

"Fine. But if you want my advice, don't wait too long, knowing he has a baby on the way with you might get him re-thinking his relationship with Alana."

"You think so?" I wondered aloud.

"Well," Simone said, "you know him better than I do, but one thing I know for sure is that it will keep his ass up late at night for a while. Wait a sec, now that I think about it, when Alana gets wind that you're knocked up, talk about a diva in turmoil. Damn, I would pay to see some shit like that. OK, I take it back; I have to be on the phone. I'll even set it up, like a conference call. Even better do this in person. When can you fly back to Chicago?"

"Simone, you're killing me," I said. "I told you 'no' already."

"Ugh, you know you are one stingy bitch sometimes."

Simone and I laughed at her silliness. I sat back in my chair and threw my feet up on the desk. My back was really starting to bother me.

"Listen," I said, "I met this guy."

"Black guy?"

"Yes, black."

"Does he know you're knocked up?" Simone asked.

"I told him."

"And he's still around?" she said with feigned surprise.

"He just wants to be friends."

"No, oh naïve one, he just realizes that he can't get you pregnant."

"No, seriously," I insisted.

"Uh huh, I am being serious, go on," Simone said.

"Anyway, there is something about him that I can't quite put my finger on."

"Hmm, let's see, a guy who still calls you even after he knows you are pregnant with another man's seed, a black man at that, and you can't quite put your finger on it. Shocker."

"OK fine," I continued, "maybe it is kind of weird. I don't know, I just get a weird vibe from him sometimes, but he is cool to talk to."

"You know, Ted Bundy was interesting to the ladies too, until they ended up raped and dead."

"OK, stop."

"Listen, I'm sure he's not a serial killer or a brother who wants a relationship for that matter," Simone said, "but be careful. Remember you're in New York, alone, pregnant, with no support system, so watch your back."

"I will, and now I'd better go, I have a new client coming in a few minutes."

"So, how's the new gig going by the way?"

"It's good," I said, "just laying my foundation like you taught me."

"That's right, follow what I say and you will rise to the top. OK, call me later. Love you."

"Love you, too, Simone," I said as I hung up the phone.

Maybe Simone is right. Maybe it is weird that Patrick isn't running for the hills after finding out that I'm pregnant. I wonder what's keeping him around?

Chapter 19
ALANA

Todd and I decided to take Riley to the park. It
was a relatively warm day in Chicago, about 72
degrees and the sun was making its way through the
abundance of clouds in the sky. Saturdays were
always a good day for Todd and I to bond, seeing that
neither of us liked to work on the weekends –
although this weekend I had something on my mind
that I needed answers to, so I figured relaxing in the
park while Riley played was the perfect opportunity
to pry.

"So Kai's in New York?" I asked, not wasting any time to get out what I needed to get out. I was never one to beat around the bush, any bush. I liked to jump right on in.

Todd was lying on his back with his eyes closed, maybe trying to get in a little nap, or maybe just resting his eyes. But once he heard her name, he sat up slowly and turned his head to look at me.

"What?" Todd asked.

"So, I hear Kai is in New York."

"Where did you hear that from?" Todd asked with a noticeable tinge of irritation in his voice.

See, that's mistake number one, I thought. Don't answer a question with a question, as that is the ultimate indication that a lie is on its way next.

"Does it matter where I heard it? Is it true?"

"Yeah, but…" he stammered.

"But what, Todd? When were you gonna tell me?" I demanded.

Todd looked away, and then back at me, shrugging his shoulders. "Why does it matter that Kai is in New York?"

"That's not the point, the point is you knew and didn't tell me."

"It's not a big deal, Alana, really. Kai is in New York, there, you happy now?" Todd snarled as he slowly lay back down on his back. "And if you're wondering, no, I haven't talked to her, someone told me, OK?"

Hm, lie number two I thought, they just keep rolling out I see.

"Really? And who is that person?" I asked.

"What is this, Alana?" asked Todd. "A twenty questions game about Kai?"

"No, just one question, the one that you failed to tell me about," I replied a smug look on my face.

Todd sighed and turned his head away, mumbling something to himself – which I freakin' hated. If you want to talk about me, I thought, think it, don't go mumbling it. "I'm sorry, did you say something?"

Todd sat back up and turned towards me. "Listen, Alana. Yes, Kai is in New York, I found out from a friend in passing, but it's not a big deal, so that's why I didn't feel the need to tell you. I mean, you should be happy she moved out of Chicago. It's one more indicator that she is out of our lives. So, can we just drop this, please?"

"Really? So she is totally out of our lives?"

"Yes, totally," Todd said.

"And you haven't talked to her?"

"Alana, I really don't know why we are even having this conversation."

I wanted to say, "Because your ass is lying and you're hiding the fact that you contacted Kai on Facebook, but clearly, just like a fucking man, you will deny it till you die or I kill you out of rage. So you force me to do what I have to do to put a stop to this my way, Alana's way." But I kept that to myself. Instead, I said, "You know what, Todd? You're right, I don't know why I brought it up either."

"Thank you. Now can I please get a little rest?" Todd asked.

"Of course," I replied with a forced smile. I bent down and planted a soft kiss on his lips.

I should have known Todd would lie about his contact with Kai, that's why I never came to the table without a Plan B. He wanted to act like Helen Keller, fine my ass could be Inspector Gadget, I thought. We all have a roll to play, goddammit.

***

The sun was starting to set and Todd and I decided to grab a quick dinner at the corner market and head home. Even though our Saturday park outing didn't pan out exactly as I planned, I was already on to Plan B.

Minutes after we got home Todd announced that he was staying in for the night to watch a movie. He wanted me to join him, but I had other things I needed to take care of. Like making sure Kai was out of our lives for good.

"So you sure you don't want to stay in and watch a movie?" he asked. "We could cuddle and stuff," he added. I quickly recognized that in his own way, he was trying to apologize for snapping at me earlier in the park.

"I would love to, but my agent wants me to hit this party where all the cast members of the movie will be. If you want to come with me, you can," I said. I was lying through my teeth but I knew Todd would pass since he hated industry parties.

"No, I think I will just stay in. Riley and I can watch a movie. Besides, we would have to find a babysitter."

"OK," I said, but what I really wanted to say was "Perfect!" I had some important shit to take care of.

The second Todd headed upstairs to jump in the shower, I whipped out Jessica's business card and dialed her number. I knew trying to see her last minute was risky, but the way her ass was sweating me, I was sure she would move her plans around to fit me in.

"Hello?" Jessica answered the phone not knowing who was calling.

"Hey, Jessica, it's Alana, Alana Brooks, remember?"

"Hey there, beautiful. To what do I owe this pleasant surprise?" Jessica asked in a very sexy tone.

Oh gawd, I thought, does this bitch ever turn it off? "Well, I've been thinking about you and wondering if you wanted to go grab a drink tonight."

"With you? Of course. Just say when and where and I will meet you."

This was gonna be easier than I thought. "How about we meet at this bar on Dearborn called Nicco's… say 8:30?"

"Perfect. I live in those lofts right upstairs from there."

"Actually, I had no idea, what a coincidence," I said. I hoped the bitch didn't think I was stalking her or anything.

"So, 8:30, I will see you there," Jessica said, confirming the time.

"OK," I said.

"Great, I can't wait to see you," Jessica said.

"Yeah," I replied, quickly hanging up the phone before she had a damn orgasm. I looked at my watch and it was 6:30, which gave me time to think about what I wanted to wear – and to come up with a good plan.

***

I got to Nicco's around 8:45 on purpose, knowing Jessica would be there already. I didn't want to seem too eager, nor give her the satisfaction of having me waiting for her. I walked into the bar to see her chatting up the bartender. Since she lived right upstairs, I imagined she knew the whole staff. I dipped into the bathroom before Jessica had a chance to see me, to do one last face and outfit check. I had decided to wear my red wrap dress with black pumps and silver jewelry. The dress accented my ass and breasts, and let's face it, this was a business call as far as I was concerned.

"Hey, Jessica," I said as I slid into the chair next to her at the bar.

"Hey beautiful, wow, don't you look stunning in your red. Did I mention red was my favorite color?" Jessica asked as she gave me a smile and a wink. I took a deep breath realizing I may have to knock this bitch out before the night is up.

"Nope, didn't realize it, I guess this is a big old fat coincidence," I said as I settled into my seat.

"As well as me living right upstairs from to the bar you picked. Some might think you were stalking me," Jessica said as she chuckled, taking a sip from her drink. I noticed her eyes never gazed anywhere other than my tits.

"Well, I wouldn't go that far," I said.

"I was happy when you called and wanted to meet for a drink, I don't get out much since I am relatively new here, ya know?" Jessica smiled as the bartender came over and placed a drink in front of me. "I ordered you a drink, pomegranate martini with extra vodka. You do drink don't you?"

"I do now," I said, thinking this woman was no joke. It was a pretty clear attempt to get my ass drunk, so I needed to work fast before that happened.

"So Jessica, what part of New York are you from?"

"I grew up in Queens, but I moved to Brooklyn right after college," she said, as she finished off her martini. She turned and flagged the bartender down indicating she wanted a second round - – or her third for all I knew.

"You must really miss New York, I mean it has to be more exciting than Chicago."

"Yeah, New York has its perks, but so does Chicago," Jessica said as she touched my leg. I crossed my right leg over my left pulling it just out of her reach. I took a sip of my drink, thinking I may have missed my window there.

"Did you leave anyone back in New York. You know, someone special?"

Jessica looked at me then turned to face the bar as she sipped seductively on her drink. "Maybe, but a girl doesn't kiss and tell, Alana. You should know that, right?"

I wanted to say, Ah no, not when I'm trying to get some damn information out of your drunk ass.

"Don't you just love the buildings on this block?" Jessica asked as she began to swivel in her chair from left to right. "This was the first place my realtor showed me and I fell in love with it immediately."

"Yeah, it's very nice," I said, but I was thinking, If you're a damn lush and want to live next to a bar, then sure, it's perfect.

"Hey, you wanna see my place? It's so damn hot and cozy."

"No, I can't stay out too late, I have an early shoot in the morning and I don't want to have those unsightly bags under my eyes," I said with a polite smile. I was beginning to think that this whole meet and greet was a big ass waste of my time.

Suddenly, all that quickly changed when Jessica's Blackberry rang on the bar and I looked down to see "Toni calling."

Hmm, what another coincidence, I thought. Jessica was so damn tipsy she didn't even notice her phone was ringing.

"Jessica, I think you're getting a call on your phone."

"Oh, thank you, beautiful," Jessica said as she quickly picked it up. "I'll make this quick," she said as she shot me a wink.

"Hello, sweetie, how are you?" Jessica sang into the phone. I was all ears, especially since I was hoping this was the same Toni I saw on Kai's Facebook page.

"Really, that sounds intriguing, details please," I heard her say. I was ear hustling so tough it was as if I had a funnel connected from my ear to Jessica's mouth. I wished I could have heard what this Toni woman was saying on the other end. I wondered to myself if she was talking about Kai.

"Wait, say again, sweetheart? It is kinda hard to hear you. I'm in the bar next-door with a new friend," Jessica said as she touched my leg again. I swore if she grazed my thigh one more time she would be pulling back a nub. "Well," she continued, "how about I head up to my place so you can hear me. Hold on."

Jessica put her phone down and directed her attention toward me. "I have to run upstairs, I can't hear my friend and she really needs to talk. You wanna just come up with me and we can finish our conversation there?"

I thought about the proposal, and really didn't want to be lured up to her place. But this could also be a good segue into talking about this Toni woman on the phone, the reason I was there in the first damn place. Fuck it, I thought, why not?

"Sure," I said as I threw down $10 for a tip as Jessica waved "bye" to all her bar buddies. We walked outside moving towards the second door down the street and headed up to her fifth floor loft.

Jessica finished her conversation with the mysterious Toni about 20 minutes later. As they talked, I busied myself with a tour of her place. She wasn't lying, her place was amazing. I would have considered living there if I could have done it without Jessica in the picture, of course. I was sitting on Jessica's , soft leather couch when she came into the living room with two glasses of wine. She had finished her conversation, but by the look on her face, she wasn't quite finished with me.

"Sorry about that, beautiful." she said as she sat close to me on the couch. "Ever since I moved to Chicago, I haven't had time to connect with my friends much back in New York," Jessica handed me my white wine.

"I see. Not to pry or anything, but was that an ex of yours?"

"An ex what?"

"Like ex-lover."

Jessica laughed. "Damn, you're so cute, you know that?" Jessica said as she leaned in to kiss me. I let her in and the next thing I knew we were in a serious lip lock on her couch. My pomegranate martini was definitely a factor in this move, because I did not come up here to have sex, but to get information. I pulled it together and pulled my body away from her.

"I didn't come up here for this Jessica, really."

"You could have fooled me." Jessica said as she continued to caress my leg, making her way to my inner thigh.

"I'm serious." I said as I moved my leg away.

"Then why did you call me?" Jessica inquired.

"Well, I um, I just thought that maybe we could, you know, talk and maybe develop a friendship," I said, although, I didn't really believe that myself.

"Is that right? Well, tell you what? You let me do what I want with you and I will tell you all my dirty little secrets, because it sounds like that's what you wanna hear."

"Why do you think I want to know your dirty little secrets?" I said getting defensive. I was surprised at how easily she had deduced my intentions.

"Because you've asked me two times about my past lovers in a matter of twenty minutes, that's why." Jessica said as she came in a bit closer.

"Call me curious I guess," I said as I felt my heart pounding a little faster.

"Then do we have a deal?"

I thought about her offer for a minute. Leaving here without any information would have defeated the whole damn purpose of meeting with this oversexed she-beast of a woman in the first place. So, what the hell? If it gave me some info to use against Kai, then so be it.

"Deal," I said with a smile.

"Oh good. I was hoping you'd see it my way." Jessica said with a huge smile on her face. She ran her hands up my legs and around to the middle of my back, and slowly crawled on top of me.

She started off by kissing me on my neck and slowly worked her way my chest, then back up again. I had to admit, she wasn't half bad. I could have given her a few pointers but why interrupt her flow?

"Tell me what you like." Jessica said, as she continued to kiss my neck on every angle she could reach. I wanted to say; I like it quick and often, but in your case just quick.

"I'm easy." I said, then thinking how that may have sounded to a woman like Jessica. I quickly corrected my sentence. "I mean, I am easy to please." I said.

"Is that right, well I'm easy to pleasure." Jessica said as she winked at me then began to raise up my dress. I wanted to ask her if she had any toys, preferably ones that resembled a penis. I like my pussy eaten as much as the next girl, but I also like to have a grand finale, if you know what I mean. Jessica wasn't the one to give it to me, but I needed to make her think she was.

Jessica finally managed to strip me down to my pink satin bra and panties and I was thinking I had better start asking some questions before it was too late.

"The woman on the phone, is that a past lover?" I asked, getting right to the point .

Jessica stopped what she was doing and looked at me. "How did you know it was a woman?"

"Well, I just assumed." I said, thinking Jessica must not be as drunk I thought if she remembered that she didn't tell me the gender on the other end. Jessica just smiled.

"Well you know what they say about assuming. Baby, let's talk later, I have too many things I want to do to you right now."

"OK, as long as we don't forget." I said trying not to sound too desperate.

"Of course," Jessica replied, and she sank down back into my body as she continued to do her thing.

Chapter 20
KAI

Patrick and I decided to hit the Museum of
Modern Art, or as it was better known to the public
MOMA. We met at the subway entrance about two
blocks from my house, then quickly jumped on the B
train and headed into Manhattan. I had always loved
riding trains. It was a great way of getting from point
A to point B without really putting too much
brainpower into it. You could sit back and just relax
and not worry about overly aggressive drivers or
bumper-to-bumper traffic.

I was gazing out the window when I felt Patrick staring at me. I turned, shifting my body toward him.

"Hey."

"What are you thinking about?" Patrick asked.

"Just how interesting New York is, and how freakin' big it is."

"Yeah, tell me about it. You have no idea just how big a city is when you have to walk from Manhattan to Brooklyn."

"And why would anyone in their right mind do that?" I asked.

"I don't think anyone wanted to, but remember in '03 when New York had that blackout? Well if you didn't walk home you weren't getting home, and I don't know about you, but I'm too much of a snob to sleep on the streets."

"How long did it take you?"

"Oh, about twelve hours or so," he continued, "give or take stopping to get some water and a snack along the way, but I, along with millions of other Brooklynites, were on a mission ."

"I can't even imagine," I said in amazement.

We got to our stop at Rockefeller Center Station, which took nearly 40 minutes by train - I could imagine how much time it would've taken to walk. Patrick and I got off the train with a dozen or so other New Yorkers and moved up to the streets where we walked a few blocks north up to 53rd.

I have always loved museums, even as a child, they were so fascinating to me. The diversity of art and creativity is so inspiring and a great way to escape.

"So what do you wanna see first?" I asked Patrick after he paid for us to get in. I looked over the brochure they gave me and looked over our options.

"Actually, I'd like to see what the café has first," Patrick said as he rubbed his stomach.

"You wanna eat already?"

"We'll need our energy to walk around this monstrous place, don't we?"

I smiled at Patrick, "OK, to the café we go. I should probably eat something as well," I said and I flipped through the directory to see exactly where the café was located.

"Yes, you should," he said. "I am only thinking of the baby, you can't starve a helpless child."

"Yeah, yeah, let's go before you start thinking I am a bad mom."

We headed towards the café was lucky enough to find a small table in the overly crowded room. Apparently everyone had the same idea of getting food before taking the art tour around MOMA. I was in the mood for something sweet, so I ordered a waffle and a few pieces of chicken sausage. Patrick on the other hand ordered a salad and side of hummus and pita bread, which I found a bit odd.

"Are we on a diet?" I inquired.

"No, not at all. This is a normal lunch for me, I'm a vegetarian."

"So how long have you been a vegetarian?" I asked as I buttered my waffle and cut it into eight sections.

"Oh, for about 10 years now. It was a choice I made when I decided to drastically turn my life around," Patrick said mysteriously as he doused his salad with balsamic vinaigrette.

"I see," I said. I had to stop myself from prying into what had made him turn his life around. Instead, I focused on my waffle instead of another unwelcome and likely intrusive question.

"Aren't you wondering why I needed to turn my life around?" Patrick asked with a smile.

"No, not at all," I said, returning his smile.

"You lie so well, Ms. Edwards."

"OK, fine, I am wondering," I said, "but only if you want to tell me."

"Well, it's not a huge deal really," Patrick said as he took another bite of his salad, washing it down with his iced tea. "I was in my teens and I was pretty heavy into drugs."

"Really, you?"

"Oh yeah," he went on, "I did some stupid things in my life that I'm not too proud of. I don't know where I would be today if my parents hadn't moved me from Chicago to Brooklyn."

"Moving to New York saved your life?"

"Well, I wouldn't necessarily say New York exactly was my savior, but getting away from the crowd I was rolling with in Chicago was."

He put down his fork and continued, "After we moved to New York, my dad made it a point to keep me away from 'that type' of crowd. He put me in a private school and made me come straight home after."

"Wow, that was probably a big change for you!"

"Definitely," he said, " it changed my life in ways I couldn't even comprehend back then. I rebelled a few times, but my dad kept putting his foot down, saying he was doing this for my own good."

"And look at you now, law school student and upstanding citizen," I said with a joking tone, but I was serious. "Your dad did a great job with you," I added.

"Well, thank you." There was a lull as we tried to figure out what to say next. I didn't have to wait long for Patrick to continue the conversation. "What about you, have you ever been tempted with drugs?"

"No, not me, but I have a family member who is still fighting that battle."

"Wow," Patrick said as he looked away.

"I guess he wasn't as lucky as you," I said, thinking about my drug-addicted brother for the first time in months. It brought sadness to me, a deep sadness.

"Are you OK?" Patrick asked, picking up my sudden mood change.

"Yeah, you just got me thinking about someone that I used to be kinda close to."

"You want to talk about it?" he asked.

"No, probably shouldn't. I'd rather keep this day upbeat, if you don't mind."

"Not at all, I'm sorry I threw my little bit of spotted history on you." Patrick said. Sensing a need to change the subject, he grabbed the brochure away from me and opened it up. "I say we hit the architectural design exhibits first." He closed the brochure and placed it back on the table.

"Architecture? Really? OK," I replied.

"Yeah, before I decided to become a lawyer I wanted to be an architect."

"Wow, why didn't you?" I asked.

"Let's call it a lack of creativity on my part."

"Can't draw a stick figure, huh?"

"Not even if the stick was provided," he laughed.

We both got a good chuckle from that as we finished up our lunch and headed for the 5th floor to view the architectural designs.

Chapter 21
ALANA

I had a 9:30am breakfast meeting with Emanuel and I was running 20 minutes late. I couldn't understand why he couldn't meet for lunch, who eats breakfast anyway? All I need is a double latte and half a bagel, and besides, lunch with a cocktail is far more exciting than scrambled eggs with OJ. I scurried into the Morning Bliss Café to see Emanuel already there and reading the morning paper.

"There you are!" Emanuel said and he neatly folded his paper, placing it on the chair next to him. "I was about to put an APB out on you."

I wanted to say, No you weren't and stop being so damn gay and dramatic, but instead I replied, "Sorry I'm late. Apparently the Chicago cab drivers didn't get the memo that Alana Brooks was in a rush this morning." I settled in the chair across from him.

"Well you look fabulous this morning," Emanuel said as he smiled from ear to ear. "But then again, when don't you look fab?"

"This is true," I said.

"I have some very good news. Another script just landed on my desk that has your name written all over it."

"Am I the lead?"

"No, but close. You would be playing opposite the lead."

"Oh, OK. Well, who's the lead?" I asked.

"Are you ready for this?" he asked with mock concern.

"Ready as I'll ever be."

"Bow-Wow," Emanuel said, as if hearing the name Bow-Wow would make my toes curl.

I sat back upon hearing the name. "Bow-Wow? Isn't he, like, twelve?"

"He's 25," Emanuel answered, "and you would be playing his mother."

A chill went down my spine and I quickly sat up straight. "Excuse me? His what?"

"His... mother?" Emanuel repeated hesitantly.

"Do I look like I could have a 25-year-old son?" I asked, raising my left eyebrow as I leaned back and crossed my arms, just daring his ass to say yes.

"Well, no, but with makeup and hair and a little tuck here and there, who knows?"

"What?" I exclaimed.

"Just kidding. Come on, you know you are stunning."

"Thank you, but no thank you," I said. "I will so pass on that opportunity."

"Sweetheart please, trust me on this one. You want to do this part. I mean let's be real, you are not Taraji Henson – yet."

"Taraji Henson didn't start off playing people's mothers either."

"No, but her last role was a mother and it got her an Oscar nomination."

"This is true..." I said, thinking Emanuel had a damn point.

"Child, just because you are playing a mother in this film doesn't mean you will be playing one for the rest of your career. As your agent I strongly advise you to consider this, and as a friend I say take the role and check your ego at the door. I mean, let's be real,

Victoria's Secret won't be knocking at your door forever."

"Whatever, bitch."

We laughed, the tension in the air dissipating.

"Don't say no just yet, OK?" Emanuel pleaded.

"Fine," I said, "I will consider it. The way my life is going right now, this offer doesn't surprise me."

"Uh oh, what's going on now? Oh wait! Please don't tell me you are still obsessing about your man and his ex," Emanuel said as he finished up his herbal tea while quickly waving down our waitress for a refill.

"Yes, I met with this woman to try to get some dirt on Kai and ended up sleeping with her."

Emanuel started to choke on his last sip of tea. "Stop the presses. You slept with yet another woman?"

"Yeah, so what?"

"So you're not a One-Time Sally. You really do swim with the fishes. Now I'm impressed."

"Well," I said, "don't get too carried away with your admiration, I was fishing for information."

"I bet you were," Emanuel said as he chuckled. "So what happened, did you catch the big one?"

"Cute, but like I said, I'm trying to get information out of this woman about this other woman who could be sleeping with Kai."

"Girlfriend," Emanuel said, "that sounds juicy, but what kind of information are you trying to get that you're willing to eat pussy for?"

"Information that will deter Todd from ever wanting to get back with Kai. Forever."

"And exactly what kind of results are you after?" he asked.

"I need proof that Kai is actually sleeping with this woman, so I can relay that back to Todd and he can see once and for all that Kai is a true blue lesbian and doesn't want anything to do with him."

"So deterring Todd from seeing Kai by telling him she is now a lesbian, by sleeping with a lesbian – is that your plan?" Emanuel asked.

"Yep," I answered.

"Really?" Emanuel said with a singe of uncertainty in his voice.

"I know this whole girl-on-girl thing with Kai is a sore spot and a deal-breaker for Todd."

"But, hello," he said, "um, you just slept with woman number two last night, so that makes you…" His voice trailed off.

"A woman with a plan and an agenda, that's what it makes me," I said flatly. "Don't get it twisted."

"Hmm, you are definitely doing the most twisting, but if you say so. Did you find anything useful?" Emanuel asked.

I fell back in my seat and rolled my eyes. "Not a damn thing," I said. "The bitch passed out after it all went down."

"Damn, don't you just hate when that happens?" Emanuel asked with a smile.

"Yeah, whatever. This is going to be harder than I thought." I said, feeling my frustration rise by the second.

Emanuel took a deep breath. "I swear, I usually don't do this, but seeing that your obsession may cost you your next movie, which in turn will cost me my commission and my trip to Aruba, I'm going to help you out, sister girl." He pulled out his Blackberry and started to scroll through it. "I have a friend in New York who can pretty much get any type of information about anyone."

"Like what?"

"Well," he continued, "in your case, like if they are playing for the other team or both."

"Is that so?" I sat up in my seat, leaning in toward him. "Tell me more."

"I can run it past him and if this woman you are investigating has slept with other women, well, he would know."

"It's that easy?" I asked.

"Child, in the straight world there are six degrees of separation, in the gay world we're talking maybe four."

"Well, then," I asked, "what do I have to do?"

"Start by getting this woman's phone number, so he can track down exactly where she lives in New York."

"Damn, if I had known this the other night I could have gotten her number out of her phone after she passed out and I'd be done with her ass."

"Well," Emanuel went on, "that's the price you pay when you don't know what you're doing."

"What is that supposed to mean?" I asked, glaring.

"Everyone knows you don't give up the goods before you get the info. I guess you will be eating a little more pussy," Emanuel said, smiling as he picked up his tea.

Chapter 22
KAI

I was watching my pregnancy DVD when I got a text from Patrick saying that he wanted to stop by for a minute. We'd had such a great time that other day at the museum that I didn't consider his unexpected visits a nuisance anymore. I texted him back that I was finishing up my workout and to come by in an hour or so. I couldn't imagine why he needed to stop by, but my day was pretty open so it was all good. I thought maybe we could go grab a bite to eat or just take a walk in the park. Either way, I decided that I liked Patrick's company and loved the fact he wasn't trying to be more than just friends.

I jumped in the shower and decided to wash my hair as well. Air-drying was going to be my look until I could find a good hairstylist to straighten this thick mane of mine.

Precisely one hour from when I texted Patrick back, he was on my doorstep ringing my doorbell.

"Hey, there," I said as I opened the door.

"Good morning. At least I hope it has been a good one for you so far," Patrick said with a smile.

"So far, so good, I can't complain," I said.

I noticed Patrick had two Styrofoam cups in his hand and he extended one my way. "I took the liberty of bringing you some coffee, decaf, of course."

"Oh, that was very sweet of you, thank you," I said as I took the coffee and we headed toward my kitchen.

"So what brings you my way this morning?" I asked. I dug into a small sugar bowl on my counter to add a little more sweetness to my decaf java. I was a "sugar-holic" which meant that everything had to taste like it was borderline diabetes serum.

"I wanted to stop by and say hello and talk to you."

"About?" I asked as I stirred in the sugar and took a few sips before it was just right.

Patrick shifted from left to right. I noticed he was a bit different today. He looked almost nervous even.

"You OK. Do you want to sit?"

"Actually," Patrick said, "maybe we can sit down in the living room, if that's OK with you."

"Sure," I said as I grabbed my coffee and we headed back into the living room.

I sat down on my couch crossed-legged as Patrick sat across from me on my matching loveseat. He leaned forward, crossing his right leg over his left.

"So, what's up, friend?" I asked, just in case Patrick was here to confess his dying love for me, although that would probably be a long shot since we had only known each other for a few weeks at that point.

Patrick took a sip of his coffee and gave me a half-smile. "Remember when we first met and I thought you looked familiar to me?"

"Yeah, and that's when I told you I was from Chicago and you kinda blew it off, not mentioning you were from there, too."

"Well," he said slowly, " because when you told me your name, I recognized it immediately, I just didn't say anything."

"What? Why?" I asked as I sat up on the couch. I didn't have a good feeling about this, not at all.

Patrick kind of shifted in his seat again. "Because you never knew me, that's why."

"I don't understand what you're getting at," I said.

"I, um, I knew your brother Raymond," he said.

Upon hearing Raymond's name come out of Patrick's mouth my body went stiff. "How... how do you know my brother Raymond?" I asked with a cautious tone.

"We used to run in the same crowd back in the day... back in Chicago."

I sat there in silence, not really knowing what to say or where this conversation was going. I let Patrick talk because clearly, he had a lot to say.

"Remember how I said I was on drugs and the reason why my dad moved me to New York?" Patrick took a deep breath and looked out of my bay window for a few seconds then slowly turned and looked back at me. "I was there that day Kai your brother sold you for drugs."

I was still, I couldn't say anything, my mouth was paralyzed, and my thoughts became scattered.

"I was the guy who pulled them off," he continued, "I knew what they were doing was wrong and I couldn't just stand and watch. I pulled them off of you so you could run. I never would have hurt you."

I just stared at Patrick. I still could not speak. My mind was trying to process how to handle this information. I started to feel dizzy.

"When I met you at Kami and Robert's party and heard the name, 'Kai Edwards,' I couldn't believe after 20 years I would ever see you again." Patrick looked down in shame. When he looked back up, he had tears in his eyes. "I'm so sorry, Kai, I really am. I wanted to say something to you the night I met you but I was in shock and thought it wasn't the right time."

I looked away, down to the floor, as tears began to swell in my eyes. Suddenly, I had a very clear memory of that day when my brother sold me for drugs, and the memory of someone pulling a boy off of me giving me the opportunity to run. And run I did. I watched my tears drop into my lap.

"Kai, I am so sorry about what they did to you," Patrick said softly.

I looked up at Patrick. I had so many things swirling around in my head, it was like a tornado on the Kansas plains.

"I think I need to be alone, please," I said, almost a whisper.

Patrick stood. "I understand. Kai, I know what I shared with you brought back unwanted feelings, but I had to tell you, it was tearing me up not to be honest with you."

I was silent. I didn't feel the need to say anything. I couldn't. I looked back down to the floor as I heard

Patrick walk toward the door, then open and close it behind him.

"Thank you," I whispered to myself. I felt sick, as if I were about to throw up. I stood to make my way to the bathroom when suddenly a sharp pain stabbed my abdomen. My legs betrayed me and before I knew it, I was crashing down to the floor, hard. I saw a white light flash around me, then nothing.

Chapter 23
ALANA

I left Jessica a message saying I wanted to see her again. I even added that I'd had a good time with her the other night. I was prepared for her to have an attitude since she had been calling me non-stop for a week and I had not returned any of her calls. But since Emanuel told me what I had to do to get the information about this mystery woman in New York, I knew I had to get back into Jessica's good graces.

Not more than 20 minutes passed before I got a return call from Jessica. I figured she would've waited at least an hour to hit me back, but damn she was on it. I dialed her number and waited for her to answer.

"Hey, I thought you forgot about me," Jessica said as I answered her call.

"Now why would I do that? I've just been very busy, that's all," I said.

"Uh huh, well, I'm glad you finally called me back."

"Of course," I replied.

"When am I going to see you again?" Jessica asked. I sat back on my couch filing my nails. I thought I was going to have to be the one to throw out the bait, but once again, Jessica beat me to the punch.

"How about in an hour?" I replied, realizing that it was still only noon. I had a meeting with Emanuel at three and I didn't want to delay my detective work any longer than I had to.

"Noon? Well, I see someone is extra excited to see me."

I chuckled at Jessica's mixed up perception of how I felt about her, even if there was something about her that did excite me. But I had bigger plans and I couldn't deviate from them right now.

"I have to be back on set tonight and I don't know when I will be free again, sweetheart," I said. Throwing in "sweetheart" was a special touch to help sell my interest in her.

"Fine" she answered. "I'm assuming my place?"

"You have assumed correctly. I will see you in about an hour, OK?"

"I'll be there," Jessica said before hanging up. I finished filing my nails as I thought, this time I have to work this so I don't end up face down in her damn bush, because that shit is so not cool.

***

I headed up to Jessica's loft and knocked on her door, and she answered wearing a pink silk mid-thigh robe and holding a glass of white wine in her hand.

"Well, hey there," Jessica cooed as she stood there with a grin on her face.

"Hey, I see you got started without me," I said as Jessica stepped to the side to let me enter. Jessica's place smelled like sweet lavender and the voice of Luther Vandross floated through the air. My first thought was, Who plays Luther anymore to get in the mood? Then again, I wasn't dealing with an ordinary woman.

Jessica closed the door behind me, followed me into her living area and sat down next to me on the couch. "Can I get you a glass of wine?"

"No, I'm good, kinda early for me."

"You sure, not even a little?" she asked.

"No, really, I'm good," I said as I slowly sat back on her couch. I glanced toward her ottoman and noticed her Blackberry sitting there. I knew I had to get that number out of there, some way, somehow.

Jessica laid her leg over mine and began to play with my hair. "I missed you, you know."

"Really? I missed you, too…" I said. I felt my body pull away the closer Jessica got.

"How much did you miss me, Alana?" Jessica asked and she leaned in a bit closer, as she began to kiss me softly on my neck. I felt her tongue gliding up and down and I had to admit, she was good at what she did since I was beginning to get turned-the-fuck on. I pulled away, trying not to get sucked in.

Jessica glided her tongue to my ear then my cheek and eventually into my mouth as we continued to kiss deeply. I felt my body tingling and my floodgates opened up and I knew I didn't want this to stop. I wanted her to eat my pussy. Jessica was starting to work her way down my chest when her Blackberry rang.

"You need to get that?" I asked in between our serious lip locks. Jessica continued to kiss me, oblivious to her ringing phone. "Jessica?"

"Shit," Jessica said as she sat up and answered her phone. "I told my office not to bother me for the next two hours." Then she said, into the phone, "Jessica McCoy. Yes, I am aware of that. OK, OK." She continued to talk with a short and abrupt tone. She put up her index finger to tell me to give her a minute as she stood and headed to the kitchen to finish her call.

I sat up and readjusted my clothes. I had to pull it together before I fell into the same trap I did the first time, when I didn't get the information I had come to get.

I heard Jessica wrap up her call and she came back into the living room. She sat down next to me and I noticed that she'd left her phone in the kitchen.

"Now where were we?" Jessica asked as she leaned back in to resume what we had started. Even though I was having a good time I had to find a way to get Toni's number out of her damn phone.

"You know what, I think I will have that glass of wine after all," I said as I stopped Jessica in mid-kiss.

"OK, well let me go get it."

"No, no I can go," I said, and jumped up before Jessica could.

"Oh, OK. Well while you're up can you freshen up my glass?"

"Of course," I said as I grabbed her glass off the side table and headed toward the kitchen.

I got into the kitchen and immediately saw Jessica's Blackberry sitting on the counter. I reached into the fridge, grabbed the wine and poured Jessica a glass. I put the bottle down and picked up her Blackberry.

"So where do you keep your wine glasses?" I called out as I started to scroll through her Blackberry searching for Toni's number, thinking it would have helped if I had known her last damn name.

"Look in the top cabinet all the way to the right, second shelf," Jessica said from the other room.

I put her Blackberry down and quickly went over to the cabinet and grabbed a wine glass, placed it on the counter. I picked her Blackberry back up and continued to search through her contacts as fast as I could. I felt my heart pounding faster and faster, thinking any minute she would turn that corner and bust my ass for snooping.

"Did you find it?" Jessica yelled from the living room, startling the shit out of me.

"Yep, sure did, thanks."

"Well, hurry up and get back in here," Jessica said.

"Be right there," I said as I continued to scroll and finally saw Toni's name. She would have a last name toward the end of the damn alphabet. I stared at the number, trying to memorize it since I didn't have any paper or pen on me. I cleared her phone book from the screen and put her Blackberry back down where I found it and headed back to the living room.

Jessica saw me coming her way and sat up. "Where are the drinks darling?"

"Oh, I um, I just realized that I have to go," I said.

"You're kidding me!" Jessica said as she sat up on the couch.

"I know, I'm sorry but I just realized that my call time is actually 1:30 not 3:30. It just fucking hit me, but I will make it up to you, I promise," I said as I grabbed my purse and headed toward the door.

"I will call you later, OK?" I said as Jessica looked at me with a 'what the fuck' look on her face.

"OK, um, bye," I said as I turned and headed out of her loft, closing the door behind me.

***

I called Emanuel to see if we could push our meeting up an hour, since I got what I needed from Jessica quicker than I thought I would. I knew I needed to stay focused. I had a plan and no woman was going to knock me off course. My name isn't Kai Edwards.

Emanuel agreed to meet me a little earlier and I was grateful, since I didn't want to sit around and wait for 3pm to come. We met at our usual restaurant and I could tell the moment Emanuel walked in that he had some good news to share, as did I.

"There she is, Miss America." Emanuel sang as he made his way across the room to where I was sitting. He was wearing a pair of tight jeans and a baby blue button up that he tucked in ever so snug. His shirt was open and for the first time I noticed that Emanuel shaved his chest.

"You look very GQ today," I said.

"Oh, thank you, darlin' and you look oh-so-fabulous as ever."

"Naturally, but thank you," I said, thinking how my hair couldn't look great since I was lying on my back at Jessica's.

"I just got off the phone with the director and he loves, loves, loves you and will probably want to work with you again."

"As a leading lady?"

"Baby steps, girlfriend, baby steps."

"Of course, right, baby fucking steps."

"But don't lose hope," he continued, "because sooner or later you will be up there with the who's who, you mark my words, girlfriend."

Emanuel continued to talk and I tried to stay focused on what was coming out of his mouth but it was damn hard, since all I wanted to do was give him this Toni woman's number so his boy could get on his job.

"Just to let you know, the tentative premiere dates of the movie are going to be in the next couple of weeks. I'll firm that up with the producer as soon as possible." Emanuel scanned through his little to-do list on his Blackberry. "Oh, and there will probably be a premiere in New York, as well as Egypt."

I felt myself in a daze, not listening to a word that was coming out of Emanuel's mouth.

"OK, what the hell is on your mind? I just said Egypt and you didn't even bat one false eyelash."

"Nothing," I said, "really."

"Spill it and don't make me hurt you."

"Well, since you asked, I got the number, you know, of that Toni woman in New York."

"Is that right?" Emanuel asked as he sat back and folded his arms.

"And I didn't have to eat any, well, you know."

"Pussy?" he smiled.

"Exactly."

"Are you disappointed about that?" Emanuel asked with a chuckle.

I ignored Emanuel's smart mouth as I whipped out a Post-It note with the number and placed it on the table between us. "I had to memorize this because I didn't have paper and pen at the time."

Emanuel took the note and put it in his front jeans pocket.

"You're not going to lose that are you?" I asked.

"Would you please relax because this little thing you have hanging over your head, I am so over it. No, I will not lose your precious number but for getting this information you have to swear to me that you will drop this whole charade once and for all."

"But..." I started to protest.

"Swear, bitch!" he demanded.

"OK, fine, I swear," I said, thinking that I probably shouldn't lie like I do.

"Now, like I was saying," Emanuel went on, "there is a premiere in New York, but I am not sure when that will take place."

He looked at his watch. "Oh, have to run, I'm off to a speed dating party."

"They have speed dating for gays?"

"Oh, yeah, honey, it's the quickest way to meet a guy, hook a guy and fuck a guy in under an hour."

"Don't they have gay night clubs for that?" I inquired.

"Those are good too, but this is better. Ciao, Bella!"

Emanuel headed out the restaurant and I felt the need to remind him one last time. "Don't forget to give the number to your friend," I called to him, because I will be damned if I step foot back into Jessica's loft again I thought as I watched him leave.

Chapter 24
KAI

I felt a soft touch and opened my eyes from a deep sleep and saw Toni standing over me. I wanted to ask her where I was and what happened but as I scanned the room I realized I was in the hospital.

"What happened?" I asked. My throat felt like it was coated with cotton balls.

"You're in the hospital," she answered. "You fainted, Kai."

"My baby?"

"Is fine. And you're fine," Toni said.

I took a deep breath of relief as I closed my eyes for a second, trying to remember the events that led up to my being there. I opened my eyes as Toni began to stroke my hair. My mind was working overtime to piece everything together.

"Patrick... told me some things..." I said, "things about my brother and my past."

"I know, he told me. He was actually the one who brought you here."

"He did?"

"Yes, and he feels horrible about what happened."

"But he helped me, he helped me when no one else would," I said between deep breaths. It was so hard to talk, as if I had run a marathon without water. I leaned over and pointed to a cup of water on my nightstand. Toni quickly picked up the cup and guided the straw into my mouth. I felt a bit of cold relief as the water trickled in my mouth and down my throat. I swallowed a bit easier the second time.

"Where is he?" I asked, meaning Patrick.

"He's in the waiting room. Did you want to see him?" Toni asked in a soft voice.

I thought about what Toni just proposed. Did I want to see Patrick? I closed my eyes and thought that maybe now wouldn't be a good idea, maybe not for a while. Hearing those words come out of his mouth made it crystal clear that I was still not over what happened to me - still not over what my brother had done to me.

"No, I can't, not now, I'm sorry."

"Hey," Toni answered, "don't be sorry, I understand. I'll tell him to hang back for a while, and give you your space."

I nodded in agreement and to say "thank you" to Toni, because she had my back and I appreciated it.

"I took your phone and called a few people for you."

"Who?"

"Your mom and dad and your best friend, Simone. Your mom is already on a flight here. I hope that was OK?"

"Yeah, sure," I said in a weak voice. I could only imagine what was going through Corrine's mind right then. She was probably a basket case.

I stared up at Toni as I rubbed my stomach with my right hand. "Thank you for being there for me. You don't realize how much it means that you are here right now."

"Hey, I will be here for you as long as you need me, OK? I'm not going anywhere anytime soon," Toni said with a smile on her face. "The doctor is going to be here in a few minutes and I think you might be able to go home tomorrow. They just want to monitor you for a night."

"Can you stay with me tonight?"

"Of course, what ever you want," Toni said. "I'm here for you."

Upon hearing those words coming from Toni, I took one more deep breath of relief, then felt myself drifting off into a deep sleep.

***

I heard my mom softly calling my name in my dream, but soon realized it was not a dream but her standing over me. I opened my eyes and instantly smelled a familiar scent - it was my mother's familiar bath splash. I focused to see her face, but everything was still blurry.

"Hello, sweetheart," Corrine said as she smiled down at me.

"Hey, mom, how long have I been sleeping?"

"You slept through the night, honey. I got here around midnight and have been here ever since."

"Where… where is Toni?" I asked scanning the room, hoping Toni was still close by.

"I sent her home. She was exhausted and there was really no need for her to be here since I was here."

She reached for the bag sitting on the table across from me. "Are you hungry? I brought you a sandwich from the deli down the street, chicken salad." I was starving I couldn't really think about food right then, I had a million other things on my mind.

"Thanks mom, but can you hand me my water first, I'm not ready to eat yet."

"Of course, here you go," Corrine said, handing me my water." You sure you don't want just a bite of your sandwich?"

"Yeah, maybe in a minute," I said, wondering what my mom could have said to Toni to make her leave.

"Is Simone coming to New York?" I asked.

"Oh, she wanted to but I told her no."

"Why?"

"Because I'm taking you home tomorrow," she said.

"Home?"

"Relax, sweetheart, only for a few weeks, so I can take care of you while you are recovering."

"But I just fainted."

"Yes, I know, but your doctor is concerned that you are putting too much stress on your body and that, of course, affects the baby. You need to be home so I can take care of you while you rest."

I knew debating that request was a loss cause, and I figured I should just let Corrine do what Corrine wanted to do.

"OK, but just for a few weeks, mom, I have a job here, you know."

"Of course, darling, and I already called them and told them what happened. They were a little surprised to hear that you were pregnant, but your boss sends his best and wishes you a speedy recovery," Corrine said as unwrapped my sandwich and set it in front of me.

"Thanks, mom," I said, wondering what my boss and colleagues were thinking right then.

I took a few bites of my sandwich as my mind slowly drifted back to Patrick and what he revealed to me. Then it hit me. Patrick knew all along where he knew me from, and that was the weirdness I'd picked up from him. What a huge coincidence that I would meet the man who saved me 20 years ago from one of the worst incidents of my life. I wondered if he'd sought me out, or if we were meant for our paths to cross one last time. I closed my eyes to think about that for a minute. Maybe his message would help me heal, I thought; and help me close that horrifying chapter in my life. I truly hoped so.

Chapter 25
ALANA

I was anxious to know if Emanuel had found out
any information on this Toni woman in New York. It
was 9:30pm and I was chilling upstairs in a nice
warm bubble bath while Todd and Riley were
downstairs watching The Princess Diaries for the 12th
time. I loved how Todd did things like that with Riley.
It made me feel even more secure about his decision
to be in our lives. I reached over to grab my
Blackberry and dialed Emanuel's number.

"Hello, darlin', how are you?" I sang out as I leaned my head back on my pink padded pillow.

"Oh, I'm good, child, just trying to get the last of the details tied up for this premiere of yours coming up."

"How is that coming?" I asked trying to sound more interested than I truly was. Although my first premiere was certain to be an exciting time, there is a time and place for everything and right now was not the time. All I cared about was knowing what he found out about Toni.

"Just let me finish up with a few things and I will call you back tomorrow with all the details," Emanuel said in a hurried fashion. I knew I needed to cut to the chase before he hung up the phone.

"OK, but what's going on with your boy?" I asked quickly.

"My boy?"

"Yes, your boy who is supposed to be getting that information for me."

I heard a small sigh on the other end of the phone. I knew I was killing Emanuel about this obsession of mine, but hey, it is what it is and if he wanted me to continue to be his client, he needed to learn how to service all my needs and make me happy.

"Girlfriend, you are killing me. Hold on a minute," Emanuel said. I heard him put his phone down as I smiled and closed my eyes. I took a deep breath and hoped that Todd wouldn't come upstairs anytime soon.

Emanuel came back to the phone. "OK," he began, "so here is the 411. She lives in Brooklyn, which I'm sure wasn't too hard to figure out, and is a law professor at NYU. She was also married for ten years but recently divorced."

"Was she married to a woman?" I asked, needing a little more clarity on the subject.

"He wasn't sure."

"What do you mean he wasn't sure? I thought this guy could get everything?" I said in a slightly irritated tone. His fee was nothing, so I guess I couldn't complain.

"Basically your boy couldn't find out about her sexual preferences, is that right?" I asked just to clarify that this information sucked.

"Child, unless this woman flies low, low under the gay-dar, there wasn't much of her sexual history available. She must not be much of a partier."

"Great, so now what?" I asked Emanuel. I felt the need to switch to a new plan right then and there.

"Now nothing, you really need to just drop this once and for all, girlfriend. I am so done with this love triangle you got going on, you have no idea. If you want to keep pursuing this, be my guest but leave me out of it, you hear?"

I shifted my body in the tub, realizing that I needed more bubbles. I wasn't satisfied with what I'd heard, not one bit, but I know to pull back when a gay man starts to read a sister the riot act.

"Fine," I said.

Emanuel continued his rant. "I mean a few Facebook e-mails does not mean he wants her back. She would have to come with a child on her hip to get that party started child, and we both know that is so not going to happen. So, for the umpteenth time, drop it!"

I let out a loud sigh. "Yeah, you're right. Right now, Todd is downstairs watching movies with Riley. He's such a good dad to her."

"My point exactly. You need to focus on bigger and better things," Emanuel added.

That was it, I thought as I sat up in the tub, Emanuel hit the nail on the head; I did need to focus on bigger and better things. I needed to get pregnant again, making it that much harder for Todd to want to leave. Why hadn't I thought of that before? Of course, I couldn't mention that to Emanuel since he was looking for me to be in at least three more films and being pregnant was not on his agenda.

"OK, you're right, I am over it," I said as I stepped out the tub and slid into my soft pink robe.

"Don't play with me," Emanuel added.

"No, seriously, I will not bring it up again, promise."

"Thank the Lord Jesus. OK child, must run. I will call you tomorrow with the details of your premiere. I'm hearing through the grapevine that it will probably be sometime next week."

"Sounds good," I said as I drained my bathwater. I hung up with Emanuel and put my phone down on the counter. A baby would put a monkey wrench in my career, but it's not like I would be out of commission forever, just a year or so, then I could jump back in. No biggie. I figured we all had to sacrifice a bit to get what we wanted in life and right then what I wanted was Todd.

Chapter 26
KAI

I had only been in Chicago for two days and my mom was already tap dancing on my last nerve. I realized that mothers just want the best for their children, but I also knew that mothers don't know when enough is enough. My doctor gave me the OK to travel but he did advise that when I got to Chicago, I should rest for a solid week, information I wish he had not shared with Corrine.

It felt weird being back in my old room, lying in my old bed. My mother was never one to throw away anything that belonged to her children. I glanced around my room as I noticed my old oak dresser with a million stickers on its side including; George Michael, Boy George and, yes, the Puerto Rican boy band, Menudo. I glanced up at old photos of me back in grammar school, my graduation picture sitting next to my numerous track ribbons and trophies. I really needed to get back into the gym after I have this child. I used to be in such good shape.

I heard voices downstairs and could only imagine it was my mom and her housekeeper bickering again over where the saltshakers should be placed on the table. To my surprise, my door swung open and Simone was standing there.

"Surprise!" Simone exclaimed with a huge smile on her face.

"Oh, my gawd, what are you doing here? You said you wouldn't be able to stop by until this evening."

"Yeah, I lied, besides did ya think I could wait until tonight to see my BFF?" Simone asked as she came over and gave me a big hug and kiss. "Well, you haven't gained hardly any weight. Jesus, are you really pregnant or did you just swallow a basketball?"

Although I was almost five months pregnant I had hardly gained any weight other than in my stomach, but everyone was telling me that the weight would come in the last two months, so get ready.

"You look amazing as usual," I said as I scanned Simone from head to toe. She was wearing a blue pinstriped pantsuit. She slipped off her jacket to reveal a sleeveless, ruffled, button-up shirt and it was so cute. Her hair was lighter than I was used to seeing it, highlights I assumed, and her skin was radiant.

"Yeah, I try to keep it together, I mean gravity isn't working with a sister these days."

"How's it going over at McKenzie and Strong?" I asked. I'd never admit it to her, but I kind of missed the good old days when Simone and I worked together.

"It is what it is, but speaking of work, I was in Molly Stinson's office the other day and what do I see laying on her desk but an invite to a movie premiere. And not just any movie premiere, Alana's movie premiere."

"Get out! So she is serious about that acting thing?"

"Apparently so, which to me is a fucking joke. But hey, if Brittany Spears can call herself an actor anyone can."

"When is the premiere?" I asked, not really caring, but curious in a way.

"Says here that it's next week," Simone said as she pulled the invite out of her pants pocket.

"You jacked Molly's invite off her desk?"

"Sure did," she said. "Molly isn't going to Alana's premiere and besides, I wanted to show it to you."

I looked at the flyer and for the first time in months I was looking at Alana's face again. Her picture on the cover was extra glamorous. Looking at her photo, it was easy to say that I was not remotely attracted to her anymore. My days with women were over with and I was kind of happy about that.

I threw the flyer down on my side dresser. There was no need to dwell on the past. It was time to move on with my life.

"Are you gonna see Todd while you are here?" Simone asked eagerly.

"You know," I replied slowly, "I've been thinking about that and I probably should. I mean, in a few months I won't be able to fly and telling him he has a son on the way is not a message you want to deliver over the phone."

"You could just post a picture on Facebook," Simone said in her nice, nasty way.

"You're so bad."

"I know."

Simone jumped up and threw on her jacket.

"Where are you going?"

"Back to work my dear. I'll be back this evening. I just wanted to swing by and say hello," Simone said as she bent over and gave me a kiss on the cheek.

"Fine. But don't forget, I'm over having one on one time with Corrine."

Simone gave me a wink and she was out the door. I glanced over to notice that Simone left Alana's flyer on my bedside table. I picked it up and looked at it for a third time. I had to laugh at where her career has taken her.

Scanning the rest of the invite, I saw that the premiere was being held at a small theater on the north side of Chicago. I placed the flyer back down on the dresser and leaned my head against the headboard. It was time to get things moving and I knew exactly what I had to do for that to happen.

Chapter 27
ALANA

I always knew the day would come when I, Alana
Brooks, would walk the red carpet. I was excited and
nervous all rolled up in one, but tonight was my night
to shine. I put the finishing touches of makeup on
before slipping into my red wrap dress and beige
pumps. I decided to wear my hair straight, bone
straight, since it made me look a lot more striking
than the curly, Goldilocks look, not to mention I loved
how I looked in pictures with my hair like that.

I turned to head downstairs, but not before my cell phone rang. I looked down to see it was Jessica calling me. My first thought was to just ignore her. I swear, she is worse than a damn man, I thought, and doesn't get the hint. It had been a few weeks since I bounced from her loft without any explanation and I really hadn't given her a second thought since which was why she was blowing up my phone. And even though my mission was complete and her involvement in my life was officially done, I grabbed my cell phone, catching her call before it rolled into voicemail. I needed to finish this once and for all.

"Hey, girl," I said as I stood in front of my full-length mirror admiring just how hot I looked.

"You just prance out my pad and then drop off the face of the earth? What's up with that?" Jessica asked. I rolled my eyes and wanted to say, I'm the actress here and would she puh-leeze stop with the damn dramatics.

"Jessica, I would love to talk right now, but I am literally on my way to my movie premiere. Can we have this conversation later?" I said, knowing good and well I wouldn't be calling her back - at least, not anytime soon.

"Wow, you not only leave me high and dry you don't even invite me to your premiere," Jessica said.

When making out my list of attendees, Jessica never once crossed my mind, probably because I would never have her and Todd in the same room together. I mean let's be real. Why would I take that chance of Jessica snapping off in front of Todd? NOT.

"I'm sorry Jessica, it must have just slipped my mind. It's not a huge movie just a small indie film." I heard Jessica sigh on the other end. I didn't have time for this.

"Let me call you back a little later, OK?"

"That depends Alana, are you actually going to call me back later?"

"Why wouldn't I?" I asked as I played with my hair then glanced at my watch, thinking I really need to wrap this conversation up.

"Maybe because you've been blowing me off for the last two weeks. I don't get ignored, Alana," Jessica said with a stern tone.

I wanted to say, 'Well there is a first time for everything, my sweet,' but figured that would just prolong our conversation with the addition of pissing her off even more than she already was.

"Jessica, you know my schedule and you know this movie is a big deal for me and that is why I haven't called you back," I said in my most convincing tone. Shit, I really was an actress.

"Cut the bullshit, Alana, if you really wanted to see me than you would make the time," Jessica said.

I stopped what I was doing for a second. The girl had a point, I thought. "Well then, Jessica, I guess you got your answer then," I said and I pressed "End" on my Blackberry and threw it in my beige leather purse. I didn't want to get shitty with her but she gave me no choice. I mean, come now, did she really think I was trying to have a relationship with her? I heard my text message alert go off and figured that it was Jessica giving me a piece of her mind. I didn't have time for her right then and I wished she would just get the hint and step the fuck off. Even though I did enjoy being with her, I had to stay focused on the bigger picture - my career and my future with Todd. I was finally over the fear that Todd would ever want Kai back, so it was time to start moving my life with Todd to the next level, and no one and nothing was going to stop me. As far as I was concerned, I saw only smooth sailing ahead.

***

Todd and I arrived at my movie premiere in true Alana style. I decided to rent a Town Car for the night and stock it with champagne and caviar. I figured a movie premiere – or, better yet, my movie premiere – didn't come every day so why not do it up right?

I stepped out into the flashing lights of photographers and found myself on top of the world. The size of the crowd that had gathered on the other

side of the black velvet rope surprised me. Then
again, Chicago was a city that didn't get a regular
taste of Hollywood.

I looked over at Todd and knew by the look on his
face that he'd rather be at home watching football, but
he was there to support me and I wanted him to know
I appreciated it. I smiled at him and placed a small
kiss on his cheek, and in return he put his hand on my
waist and pulled me in closer.

Ever since my idea about having another baby, I
toyed with the best time to bring it up to Todd, but I
still had time and a subject as delicate as this needed
to be brought up when the time was right. I grabbed
Todd's hand and we walked the red carpet, stopping
and posing for numerous photographers as they called
out my name. I wondered if my picture would ever
see the light of day on any magazine or newspaper
stand. Even if it didn't, I was OK with the spotlight I
had in the moment. Soon enough, the whole world
would know the name Alana Brooks. We headed into
the theater where we took in our surroundings.

"So who is the young actor being bombarded by
reporters and photographers?" Todd asked as he
looked over at the commotion.

"That's Devin Gill, the director of the film."

"He looks like he's about 12."

"Actually, I think he's about 26, but he told me while we were on set that he's been shooting movies ever since he was a teenager."

"Wow, that's pretty impressive," Todd said as he took two white wines off the tray of a passing hostess, giving one to me then raising his glass. "To you, baby, on your first of many, many movie premieres."

"I'll toast to that," I said as I raised my glass, clinking it against Todd's before taking a sip.

I wasn't sure what we should be doing since no one was really clamoring to interview me. I wanted to yell out, Hello, I'm in the movie, too, and a Victoria's Secret model to boot, but I decided to stay quiet and soak in the atmosphere. My time would come soon enough.

"Do you want to go grab our seats?" Todd asked as we stood in the middle of the lobby amidst the hustle and bustle of the premiere crowd.

"No, let's stay out here for a minute, and walk in when everyone is sitting, that way I'm sure to be noticed," I said as I gave Todd a wink.

"Ah, I see. Fashionably late to your seat," Todd replied with a hint of sarcasm in his voice.

"Now you're catching on," I said and I began to scan the crowd just to see if I recognized anyone I knew. Suddenly, I saw a face that looked familiar, very familiar. The theater lobby was starting to get a bit more crowded as people from outside were heading in to take their seats. I looked again and this time I got a better look, and in that moment my stomach did a small flip as I realized I was looking at Kai.

The first thing I thought was, <u>what is that bitch doing in Chicago, let alone at my damn premiere?</u> I glanced over at Todd, who was looking in the opposite direction. Then I thought, did Todd's ass tell Kai about my premiere? What the fuck was going on? I looked again, just to make sure my mind wasn't playing tricks on me, especially since I'd had a few drinks in the car on our way over. Nope, it was her. This was the third time I had looked at her, and she looked back at me and a smile slowly crawled across her face.

I grabbed Todd's arm hard. "Did you invite Kai?" I asked.

Todd snapped his head around upon hearing her name. "What?"

"Kai is here, did you invite her?" I asked with a serious tone in my voice to let him know that this was not the time to lie.

"No, why would I do that?"

"Because she's here," I said.

"What? Where?"

Right when Todd finished his last syllable we both looked up to see Kai standing five feet in front of us. She and I locked eyes before I slowly glanced down to see something that blew me away. This bitch was pregnant! What the fuck!

"Hey, Todd, hey Alana," Kai said as she rubbed her small but round stomach about the size of an NBA basketball.

Todd and I just stood there and for the first time in my life, I was fucking speechless.

"I'm sure you're both wondering how this happened…"

I didn't know what to say, and as I glanced over at Todd who looked sick to his stomach, it was clear he didn't know what to say either.

Kai continued to prattle on, "…since we all thought I could never get pregnant. But surprise, surprise, I did! Five months ago to be exact."

"You're… you're pregnant…?" Todd managed to sputter.

"Aren't you the observant one? You'll love this, guess who the father is?" Kai asked him with a smile.

Todd turned to look at Alana then back at me. "Me?" Todd asked in a timid almost sheepish tone, his eyes the size of saucers.

"Yep. Congratulations, it's a boy," Kai said with a huge grin on her face.

I felt my body break out into a cold sweat. I wanted to swing out and hit the bitch but…she was pregnant.

"This is impossible," I said, finally uttering my first three words.

"No, Alana, what's impossible is you thinking you could get away with screwing me over."

I looked over at Todd who was motionless. For a second it looked as if he had stopped breathing. Me on the other hand, I felt like I was about to lose the caviar I had on the ride over.

I slowly glanced around the theater to see if anyone else was privy to the event that was going on in front of us, but no one seemed to be interested in our drama but us. I stared at Kai. This felt like a nightmare.

"Well, I see you two have a lot to process, so I'm just gonna go," Kai said as she turned to leave, but not before turning back around. "Oh, where are my manners? Congratulations Alana on your movie premiere, but then again, acting like a whore shouldn't be too much of a stretch for you. Bye now," Kai said. She turned and waddled her ass right out of the theater.

Just when I thought Todd and I were in the clear, Kai swoops in and drops this drama on us. I knew at that moment that I had to shift my game into high gear because shit was about to hit the motherfucking fan.

Part Two

WHEN IT RAINS IT POURS

Chapter 28
TODD

I was in pure and utter shock. I couldn't even tell
you what Alana's movie was about because ever since
Kai walked out that theater my mind was in a
different time zone. Alana was in her own personal
hell as well, but then again, Kai had dropped an
atomic bomb on both of us and just walked away
before the pieces even had a chance to land. I tried
calling Kai's cell phone after the premiere was over
but every time it rolled into voicemail. I honestly

didn't think Kai would pick up her phone but it didn't stop me from trying.

Needless to say Alana and I rode home in complete silence. As far as I was concerned, Alana's premiere night turned out to be one of the worst nights of my life and I'm sure by the look on Alana's face she would agree. I didn't know what to say or think or even feel, for that matter. I was numb and confused and I needed answers. I lay my head back on the black leather seat as I listened to the sounds of the car gliding over the concrete road. Kai was pregnant and it's mine, but how? She told me she couldn't have kids. Was she lying all along? Did she not really want kids? So many unanswered questions were swimming in my head. I opened my eyes to see Alana staring at me. Her stare was deep as if she were processing, calculating, plotting.

Alana finally broke her silence. "She's lying, Kai is fucking lying."

I pulled my head up from the headrest. "What do you mean she's lying? We both saw that damn bulge in her stomach Alana," I said. I shook my head at Alana's far-fetched assessment.

"But how do we know it's yours?"

"We don't, but the fact that she is pregnant raises a strong possibility that it could be."

Alana rolled her eyes and looked out the window. "I knew that bitch was going to try something like this." She looked back at me. "You knew about this, didn't you?"

"What?"

"Don't lie to me Todd, not now."

"How would I have known Kai was pregnant?" I protested.

"I don't know, maybe because you have been communicating with her on Facebook and lying about shit, that's why," Alana said with much venom in her voice.

I stared at Alana, trying to put what she just said into perspective. Had she been snooping around on my account? "Don't tell me you broke into my Facebook account."

"I didn't have to break in, Todd, you damn near left an open invitation with a welcoming committee for me to snoop."

"What the hell is wrong with you," I exclaimed furiously, "going into my computer and reading my emails?"

"Well, I wouldn't have to if you were fucking honest with me," Alana replied. "I asked you to your face if you were in touch with Kai and you said no."

I dropped my head. I couldn't believe what I was hearing; this night was just getting crazier by the minute. "Alana, it's not a damn crime to be friends with a person on Facebook."

"It is when you used to fuck her."

I took a deep breath and laughed to keep myself from totally exploding on her. "Well," I said, "you would know more about that than I would, now wouldn't you?" I felt my body temperature rise.

Alana and I became quiet. I had to calm down before I started wanting to hurt her ass. I'd never hit a woman in my life, but this could be a first. My mind kept shifting back to Kai, wondering if she were actually carrying my child, my son. Damn. This is so not happening right now, I told myself.

"So, Todd, what are you going to do?" Alana asked as she gave me a serious look.

"What do you mean?"

"I mean," she said deliberately, "are you going to leave me for her now?"

"What?"

"I mean, you left her for me when I told you Riley was yours?"

"Jesus, Alana, would you stop putting the carriage before the damn horse already?"

"Well, what do you expect me to think? Alana asked, her voice began to tremble.

"Can I please just process this one night before you start planning my whole damn future?" I inquired as I rubbed my sweaty palm on my tuxedo pants. "I need to talk to Kai and see what is really going on, OK?"

"Right, of course," Alana said. She looked out the window again as she shook her head. "That bitch is only doing this to get back at me, and she's not going to win."

I was startled to hear Alana's last statement. "Alana, this isn't a game, OK, this is our lives."

"Well, our lives are about to get real fucked up if she is carrying your child. I mean, let's be real. What if she is? What do you plan on doing about that?" Alana asked again.

"Listen, like I said, I can't even think that far yet, OK? And frankly, I really wish you would just let me handle this. Fuck!! I need some air," I said as I noticed we had pulled up in front of our condo. I jumped out of the Town Car and headed inside the building. My head was swirling and I needed to talk to Kai. I tried her phone one last time but it went straight into voicemail again. This time I left her a message saying I really needed to talk to her. I hit "End" and headed into the house to take a long, hot shower.

***

As Todd headed into the condo I couldn't believe how quickly the best night of my life had turned into the worst! Who did that bitch think she was, walking in and dropping that news on us and then waltzing out without so much as a howdoyoudo? Kai thinks she's got me, but what she doesn't know is that I will not be defeated. I needed to find out if that baby really was Todd's and not from some sperm bank donor. I picked up my cell phone to call in a huge favor. Kai may have dropped a bomb tonight, I told myself, but she won't know what explosives are until she sees me coming to claim what is mine. I didn't care if the bitch was pregnant. I thought, I'll be damned if she's going to get her claws back into Todd.

Chapter 29
KAI

I woke up the next morning and immediately
glanced at my phone. A message was waiting for me
and I leaned over to grab my phone and check my
voicemail. Todd had called six times last night after
my little bombshell. I shouldn't be too surprised
seeing how I left the scene of the crime the way I did.
I knew what I had done was pretty bad – OK, it was
downright scandalous – but, I felt good, really good.
They both had it coming and while they marinated on
the new information, I finally felt like I had regained

some control over my life. I figured it was time to call Todd back. He had suffered enough, not to mention the few millions questions he had for me as well. I grabbed my phone and dialed Todd's number. He picked up on the very first ring.

"Hey, Kai," Todd said in a serious tone.

"Hey, how are you?" I asked. I could feel the tension through the phone and for a few minutes we were both at a loss for words.

"Not too good Kai. You dropped some pretty big news on us last night." Todd said, letting out a huge sigh at the end of the statement.

Yeah, I did, I thought, and I could address his comment, but why? I had done what I did for a reason and to backpedal now would have just sounded stupid.

"I'm sure you'll agree we need to talk," I said.

"Yeah, we do, so when are you available?" Todd asked with urgency in his voice.

"My schedule is open all day, what's good for you?" I asked, placing the ball back in his court. I wanted to see just how urgent this was for him.

"Noon works for me, and I'm headed to the office now," Todd said.

Seeing as it was only 10am, that proved to me that Todd thought it was pretty urgent.

"That's fine, but can we do it somewhere on the south side? I'm staying with my mom."

"Right," he said. "Well, how about Park 52 in Hyde Park?"

"That sounds like a plan. I'll see you at noon."

"OK. Oh, hey, Kai?"

"Yeah?"

"How are you getting there, I mean, are you driving or taking the train?" Todd asked.

"Probably the train, why?"

"Oh... I just... well... will you be OK doing that? I mean, being pregnant and all?" Todd asked in a hesitant voice. I was a little taken aback by his concern, but it was sweet.

"Yeah, I will be fine. The walking will be good exercise," I said and a smile crawled across my face. "I've got to go, but I'll see you at noon."

"Yeah, sounds good," Todd said.

I hung up the phone and sat there for a minute thinking about what Todd must be feeling and wondered how our conversation would go. I felt a bit relieved in a way that Todd finally knew I was pregnant with his child and was willing to talk to me, although I should probably wait to see how our conversation went before I assumed anything else.

I glanced at the clock and noticed it was almost 10:30am. I needed to get up and jump in the shower. It had been a week since I'd been in Chicago and I was ready to get out and get some fresh air and a little bit of sunshine. I swung my feet around and the moment they hit the floor my phone was ringing. I looked down to see that it was Simone and I knew exactly why she was calling.

"Hey, Simone."

"I cannot believe you went to that premiere and dropped the pregnancy bomb without me!" Simone said as I laughed out loud. I left Simone a message on my way over to the theater telling her I had decided to tell Todd and Alana about the pregnancy in person.

"Yeah, I'm sorry, but if I had waited too much longer I would have lost the nerve."

"How did you know where it was? Simone said.

"You left the flyer at my house, remember?"

"I sure did and the fact that you still didn't take my ass is so wrong. You know I live for shit like that."

"I didn't want it to seem like this big production, me walking in with you. I wanted to keep it simple. Slip in and slip out."

"Yeah, leaving the place in shambles on your way out."

"Exactly, and we both know how you can get sometimes, wanting to add in your two cents. It was crazy enough as it was." I said.

"Uh, huh, I bet. So tell me what happened and don't even think about leaving out any details. Wait a sec, let me grab my damn Doritos," Simone said as I heard her crack open a bag on the other end. My friend was too much.

"You're going to kill me, but I have to call you back."

"What? No!!"

"Yeah, I have to meet Todd at Park 52 at noon."

"Oh, I am free at noon," Simone added.

"Simone, do not show up, just meet me afterwards and I promise I will tell you everything."

"OK, fine, you sure know how to make a sister beg. See you this afternoon," Simone said.

"I will call you when I'm done. Bye."

I hung up the phone and immediately started thinking of what I to wear. My stomach was making it difficult to wear regular clothing and I had yet to purchase any maternity wear. I grabbed a pink baby doll top and a pair of brown linen slacks. That should work and look cute at the same time. I wanted to get going before Corrine got back from her morning women's club meeting. I'm sure she would have a lot to say knowing I was on my way to meet Todd.

Chapter 30
TODD

I left the house before Alana had a chance to wake up. I didn't want to have another angry, paranoid conversation with her again about Kai. I needed to get some clarity before I dealt with her. I could understand Alana's concern, but for some odd reason, she seemed overly obsessed about this whole Kai situation, almost like she was hiding something herself. But I couldn't worry about that right now, I had to focus on Kai and the baby.

Damn, I thought, I cannot believe Kai is pregnant and possibly with my child – this is crazy.

I got to the office around 8:45am and noticed Maceo was walking in at the same time. I gave him a nod and he returned one back to me. I entered my office only to notice he was right behind me.

"Yo, what's up? I got a call from one of my girls saying that some shit went down at the premiere last night."

I took my suit jacket off and hung it on the back of my chair before settling into it. I threw my head back and let out a huge sigh. "Yeah, it was real messed up."

"What the fuck happened? Talk to your boy."

I rubbed my stubble on my face face with my hand. I hadn't even shaved that morning, that's how serious I was about getting out of the house before Alana woke up.

"Kai showed up at Alana's premiere last night, pregnant."

"Get the fuck outta here." Maceo said as he slowly sat down in front of me. "You're joking, right?"

"No, I wish I was."

"Is it yours?" Maceo asked.

"She said it is, but I don't know for sure. I mean, I haven't seen Kai for months and she is saying that she is five months pregnant."

"Yo, so maybe the baby's not yours."

"No, we slept together about a month before that, right around the time I found out about her and Alana."

"Damn, and we both know a bitch can't get another bitch pregnant," Maceo stated this as if he were helping to simplify things for me.

"I don't know what the hell to do," I said

"Well, where is Kai now?"

"At her mom's."

"I thought she lived in New York?"

"She does, but apparently she came back to Chicago just to tell me she was pregnant," I said.

"Fuck, I guess a text message would have been a bit too impersonal," Maceo said.

I took another deep breath. "And of course Alana is flipping the hell out, so it is just all crazy right now."

"Listen, this kind of shit happens all the time, and half the time the baby isn't even the guy's. Yo, if you want my advice, get a paternity test from both of your so-called baby mama's, that's what I would do first and foremost. I mean why put yourself through all this stress and come to find out that little bastard isn't even yours? Shit, Kanye was on point with his gold-digger song." Maceo began to sing a line from a Kanye West song, "18 years, 18 years and after 18 years he found out it wasn't his."

I had to laugh at Maceo's logic. But he had a point.

"You're not a broke motherfucker, you got a lot going on including your own practice that is doing well, so don't just take these bitches' word for it, get your proof yo."

"Well, I already saw the paternity test from Alana."

"So you have the original?"

"She actually gave me a copy of it."

"A copy? Fuck that, you need the original. Matter of fact, don't even ask her for it, you don't want to raise any red flags with her, just go get another one. All you gotta do is, when Riley is asleep, pluck out a few strands of hair and take that shit to the lab, my brother."

"You sound like you've done this before."

"A brother's gotta do what a brother's gotta do. Now, when are you going to talk to Kai again?"

"I'm meeting her for lunch at noon."

"Cool, so when you see her, tell her you will be behind her 100% – once you get a paternity test from her ass."

I had to laugh. Maceo was cracking me up.

"Don't laugh, this is your life! Take control! Shit!" Maceo said as he started singing again, '18 years, and 18 years.' The last thing you want to be doing is throwing out your hard earned chips for some other motherfucker's seeds, that shit ain't cool, yo."

"So just ask her for it?'

"Yep, and if she says no, then you're off the hook. Hell, you asked. She can't blame you for wanting to be sure. I mean for all you know Kai could have gone out and had some 'revenge sex' and got her ass knocked up and now she needs you and your money to help her raise her so called 'mistake'."

"You do have a point," I said.

"Damn right I do." Maceo looked at his watch. "Oh shit, I gotta run, I'm in court in 30. But hit me up after your lunch with Kai and remember, get that damn test," Maceo said as he headed out my office singing Kanye's song, "Gold Diggers."

I lay my head back onto my leather chair and leaned back as far as the springs would allow. It all felt like a bad dream, but deep down inside, I was hoping that maybe, just maybe, that child was mine.

Chapter 31
KAI

I jumped off the train at the 53rd Street exit, in the heart of Hyde Park. The metro was the best means of transportation if you were coming in from the south suburbs. Unlike New York, where the subway runs every 5 or 10 minutes, the metro in Chicago comes every half hour or so – a bit of trivia I had forgotten before heading to the station.

I walked down the stairs and through the underpass where I landed on the corner of 53rd and Hyde Park Boulevard. As I stood there waiting for the streetlight to change, I couldn't help but admire how diverse and artistic Hyde Park was, especially the various murals that covered the brick walls near the train station. Hyde Park was also the former residence of our newly elected president, Barack Obama. I smiled at the feeling of knowing that I was back home. I saw Park 52 about a block down and I strolled down the sidewalk without a care in the world.

Upon entering I noticed the restaurant was starting to fill up with the lunch rush. I scanned the 1,000-square-foot area and noticed that I had beaten Todd there.

"Welcome to Park 52, are you dining in or picking up?" the hostess asked as I approached her.

"Actually I will be dining in," I said with a smile.

"How many?"

"Oh, just two and I believe I am the first to arrive," I said scanning the restaurant one last time for Todd.

"Great! I can go ahead and seat you while you wait for your guest to arrive," the hostess said as she sat me in a small booth near the window. She quickly brought a basket of bread and glass of water. I wondered if she were that efficient with all her customers or just me, since she clearly noticed I was pregnant.

I was very nervous as I waited for Todd to join me. I sipped on a hot raspberry tea to calm me down a bit. Todd was usually pretty prompt, but I knew he had a lot going on so I gave him the benefit of the doubt. Finally, I looked up to see Todd entering the restaurant as the hostess pointed him in my direction.

Todd was wearing a blue suit with a white shirt and maroon tie. He looked very handsome, even with the stubble on his face.

"Hey, sorry I'm late, the parking over here is the worst around lunch time," Todd said as he pulled out the chair across from me and sat down. He cleared his throat and looked around for our waitress.

"Has anyone come to the table yet?" Todd asked, probably in need of a mid-day cocktail.

"Yeah, but I'm sure she will be back very soon."

"Right, of course," Todd said with a smile. "Thanks for meeting with me," he continued as he smoothed down his tie with his right hand.

"Of course, I, um, well, that was one of my things to do when I was in Chicago."

"How long are you here for?"

"Until next week," I said. I noticed neither one of us wanted to broach the fact as to why we were really there.

The waitress finally came back over and Todd ordered a vodka gimlet on the rocks. He was very nervous and so was I.

"I guess we need to talk about this, huh?" I said, breaking the ice.

"Yeah, that's kind of an understatement, Kai." Todd said trying to sound calm but I knew he was anxious as hell.

"Where should we begin?" I asked, immediately wishing I had said something else.. Todd shifted in his seat as the waitress brought him his drink. He immediately drank three quarters of it in one gulp. He placed the glass down and looked me directly in the eye.

"Why are you just telling me now that you're five months pregnant?" Todd asked. I guessed that he'd gotten a dose of instant courage with that shot of vodka he just downed. If I could have had a drink I would have been right there with him.

"Well, it's not that simple," I said, looking down at the piece of bread that I had buttered before Todd walked in, then back up at him.

"It seems pretty simple to me, Kai, you get pregnant, you tell the father., Or am I not really the father?" Todd asked.

I had to chuckle. I knew that question would come up. It always came up when a guy was confronted with a pregnancy.

"Who else's baby would it be? Alana's?" I said, the sarcasm dripping off my tone.

There was another awkward silence and we both looked away from each other to gather our thoughts.

"Listen Kai, I didn't come here to fight, really. I just wanted to get some answers and a bit more clarification on the matter."

"OK, what do you want to know?" I demanded..

"For starters, now that you are pregnant, do you plan on staying in New York?" Todd asked. I thought that was an interesting question to start with. I thought he would start with something like, "Do you plan on keeping it?" or, "How did you even get pregnant?" – seeing as how I told him I couldn't.

"I don't see why I wouldn't stay in New York. I mean it's not like we are together or anything, so why run back to Chicago just because I'm pregnant?"

"Right, well, I am willing to support whatever you do 100%."

"That's really nice to hear Todd," I said, although I knew that was Todd's M.O.. He was always going to be the responsible one.

"I think, though, I would feel a lot better if, well…" Todd hesitated, as if uncertain how to continue. "If I could see a paternity test."

"A what?"

"I'm sure you can understand, that this is a huge shock for me and I just want to make sure that what you say is true."

"You think I flew all the way to Chicago and showed up at Alana's premiere to tell you that I think I'm sure this is your baby? You are some piece of work, Todd Daniels," I said, and I stood up, not wanting to talk to him anymore. I turned to leave when Todd stood and grabbed my arm.

"Kai, don't leave, please. I don't want our conversation to end like this," Todd said, his eyes pleading with me. It was the first emotion he had shown since he got to the restaurant.

I slowly sat back down.

"Listen, I just think with a test it would make everything that much easier," Todd continued with his logic.

I thought about it, and if that would make Todd feel more secure about the whole situation, then fine, I would give him a paternity test. "OK, I'll get one."

"Thank you," Todd said as he drank a few more sips from his drink. "How are you feeling?"

"I'm good, thanks." I said flatly.

Todd let out a nervous laugh.

"What's so funny?" I asked.

"I'm freaking out. I cannot believe we are even having this conversation."

"Why not?"

"Because Kai, I didn't think you could even have kids," he said.

"I didn't either," I replied, " That's what made this such a blessing."

"Yeah, I guess you're right."

"How is Alana taking the news?" I asked. I had told myself I wasn't going to bring her name up, it just slipped out.

"I don't even want to go there right now," Todd said and he flagged our waitress down to order another drink.

"Should I dare ask how you guys are doing?" I asked, not quite believing myself that I was even going there.

Todd was quiet. He looked down then back up into my eyes before answering. "Yeah. Yeah, we are taking it one day at a time."

I swallowed hard upon hearing that. I guess I wasn't prepared to hear that they were doing well. But then again, I thought, what else was he going to say?

"As far as me and Alana…"

"Listen, you don't even have to go there, really. It is what it is. My main thing was to tell you about your child and well, that's what I did." I said realizing I had opened the door to talk about Alana. I thought I should close it before the conversation continued too far down that path.

"Yeah, I guess it is," Todd said with a half-smile.

Todd and I finished our lunch and I headed out of Park 52 as we parted ways with a friendly hug. I had to meet Simone down the street at Starbucks and Todd had to get back to his office. Before we parted ways, though, I let Todd know that as soon as my doctor approved the test I would get that paperwork back to him.

A small tear fell from my eye, which was only ironic because of how this all started with me dropping the bomb on Todd and Alana — but for some reason, I felt as if a bomb had been dropped on me, a bomb whose lingering after effect would be that I'll be on my own when it comes to raising my newborn son.

Chapter 32
KAI

I landed back in New York and headed straight to my therapist's office. I hadn't seen Dr. Albright in a while and I knew after what had transpired in the last couple of weeks in Chicago, I was overdue.

"It's been a while, Kai," Dr. Albright said as she smiled at me with that familiar warm smile.

"Yeah, I know I haven't been keeping up with my appointments. I had been thinking I was fine, but I'm not."

"What's been going on?" Dr. Albright asked as she adjusted her glasses and picked up her yellow pad, placing it in her lap.

I took a deep breath and thought, Wow, what hasn't been going on? So much had happened since my last visit; a million things were swirling around in my head. "Man, I really don't know where to start," I said as I lay on my back with my arms crossed over my chest.

"Try starting with what's the heaviest on your mind," she said as she sat patiently waiting for me to begin.

I repeated in my head what Dr. Albright just said, "What's heaviest on my mind." I shifted my body towards her and let out a huge smile. "Thank you."

"For what?"

"For not saying, 'start at the beginning,' because my life isn't that simple, you know?"

"I'm a therapist, Kai," Dr. Albright answered. "You wouldn't be here if it was."

I lay back onto my back again as I took a deep breath. "Well, Doc, I'm going to be a single mom." I said and for the first time the idea of that really sunk in.

"OK."

"OK? This is a big deal," I said.

"Kai, there is nothing wrong with being a single mom, it's just a little more challenging. Let me ask you, why do you think you will have to do this alone?"

"I saw Todd while I was in Chicago and I told him that he was going to be a father."

"And how did he take it?"

"Well, let's just say he took it very nonchalantly. Then again," I continued, "if I know Todd the way I think I do, he is probably processing this right now."

"It sounds like you wanted him to process this differently than how he did," Dr. Albright said.

"I don't know, maybe I just wanted him to respond to this baby like he did when he found out Riley was his child."

"He didn't take responsibility?"

"In a way, yes, although he wants to get a paternity test."

"And how did that make you feel?" the doctor asked.

I was silent, as I never had a quick comeback to the "How did that make you feel?" questions. "I guess it's only normal to want to be 100% sure, but it just seemed a bit disconcerting," I said, hoping I used the right word to express my point.

"Did you expect him to leave Alana and come back to you upon hearing the news?"

"No," I said, although I really wanted to say, "Yes," but I couldn't in that moment - probably because my reasoning for that was pure ego.

Honestly, I didn't know if I wanted Todd back, or if I just didn't want him with that conniving bitch, Alana. He is way too good for her, I thought.

"No?" Dr. Albridge repeated my answer.

I took a deep breath. "No," I said again.

Dr. Albright nodded her head before writing on her yellow pad. She wrote for a few minutes, which made me a bit uncomfortable. Maybe she could sense that I was lying, but then again, she was a therapist, not a psychic. Either way, it made me feel uncomfortable. I turned to her. "I'm lying."

Dr. Albright stopped writing. "Go on," she said as she put her pen down.

"I did expect him to want to leave her for me, or at least say he was thinking about it, but he just sat there and asked for a paternity test. We were together for three years and all he gave me was a request for a fucking paternity test."

Dr. Albright was silent. She stared at me for a moment before slipping off her glasses.

"Kai, everyone has their way of dealing with change and Todd is no different. Just because you revealed to him that you were pregnant with his child doesn't mean he should react in the same way he did when he found out Riley was his. No situation is ever the same. Understand that Todd will likely come around; he just has a lot to process right now.

Remember, you've had 5 months to process what you just laid on him a few days ago, give him some time."

Dr. Albright was right, she was always right. I guess that was why I was paying her $150.00 an hour.

Before my hour was up we did touch upon my past with Raymond, which brought up my situation with Patrick. Dr. Albright expressed to me that there was a lot more work that needed to be done with that, something we needed to start integrating within our talk session about Todd and Alana. I agreed. It was hard to bring up that part of me, but I knew the more I kept it bottled up inside the worse it would be. I said my goodbyes to Dr. Albright and promised I wouldn't let more than two weeks go by without coming back to see her. I truly didn't realize how much our sessions helped until they were done.

I headed home and the moment I walked into my apartment my cell phone was ringing. It was Toni. She must have seen me coming up the stairs.

"Hey there, neighbor," I said, happy to hear her voice. Toni was such a comfort in my life.

"Hey, welcome back," Toni, said. "I missed you!"

"You did?" I said in a playful tone, "I kinda missed you too."

"Well, that's nice to hear, I'm usually the one always doing the missing. I'm kind of a sap like that."

I closed my door behind me and felt like some company. "Hey, if you're not doing anything right now I sure could use some company," I said as I placed my bags down in the foyer.

"Why don't you come up here? I just made a big old pot of Chicken and dumplings and I'm sure you're hungry."

"You know me too well," I said with a laugh. "I'll be right up."

I did a quick scan of my place just to make sure everything was still intact before heading up to Toni's place. As I climbed the two flights of stairs I realized that I had never been up there, that she always came down to me, so I was curious to see her space.

Toni greeted me at the door with a warm smile and a soft hug. We embraced and I felt all warm and fuzzy inside.

"How you doing?" Toni asked as we pulled away from each other.

"I'm better now," I said with a smile.

"Well, come on in now, I need to feed you."

"It smells wonderful in here," I said as I headed towards Toni's kitchen. Toni place was a lot different than mine, starting with the mahogany floors and bay arched windows. It seemed bigger, as well, and she had an outside balcony that stretched across the back of her place, something I didn't have in mine.

"How are you?" she asked.

"I'm good, really good. Nothing like a little R&R to do the trick."

"Your mom let you get some rest?"

"Well," I replied, "as much as Corrine could muster." We had a good chuckle with that one.

"So did you see Todd?" she asked.

"Oh, boy, did I ever."

Toni put a bowl of dumplings and a glass of water in front of me. "That doesn't sound too good."

"It is what it is. This trip really solidified for me that I may be doing this on my own, you know?"

Toni sat down across from me. "Well, you won't be the first, and just know that you will survive it. Not to mention you have me right upstairs to be at your beck and call. I'm talking Lamaze classes, babysitter, night sitter, you name it and I'm on it. I love babies," Toni said with a smile as she reached out and touched my hand. "Bottom line is you're not alone."

"Thanks, that means a lot to me."

"Also, Kai, know that babies are blessings from God, and there's a reason you're bringing this little one into the world. Just remember that it's all good, mama."

"Yeah, I have to keep telling myself that, ya know, but it gets hard sometimes, scary even."

"Well," Toni went on, " know that, from this day forward, I'm here for you. Matter of fact what's up with a baby shower for you? We have to get you some gifts, you can't buy everything now."

I smiled as I ate my dumplings. I felt like I was home for sure.

"Simone is working on it and I have friends willing to fly in so I can have it here in New York. And after the baby is born I will fly back to Chicago and have a shower there."

"That's good," she said. "Well as far as the baby shower here, I will do my part. We can even have it outside on my balcony. I am a real pro when it comes to decorations."

"Good, cause I'm not," I said as we laughed, ate and enjoyed each other's company. In that moment, my fears of loneliness were a fading thought of the past, for right at that moment I felt loved – and ready to take on any challenge coming my way.

Chapter 33
ALANA

I had just dropped Riley off at the babysitters and was heading to my Victoria's Secret shoot when my cell phone rang. I was hoping it was Todd since I had been trying to call him all day, but for some reason I kept getting his voicemail. Our relationship had been strained ever since Kai paid us that little visit at my movie premiere and I was not happy about that, not one freaking bit. I looked down to see it was my agent, Emanuel..

"Hey, Emanuel," I said

"Darlin', I have some great news," Emanuel sang like a diva into the phone. "Are you ready for this?" he asked.

"Honey, you know Alana is ready for anything," I said, although to the contrary, I wasn't at all ready after being informed that Kai was pregnant with Todd's baby.

"I just booked your next movie. It's shooting in New York next month and get this, it's a supporting role!"

"Is that right?" I said. "When I'm in New York can I kill Kai?"

"Girlfriend," he replied, "I thought that chapter in your life was closed, never to be read again."

"Well, it was until Kai showed up at my movie premiere, pregnant, claiming its Todd's baby."

"Oh, no, she didn't!"

"Oh, yes, she did," I said, mirroring Emanuel's sentiment.

"Child, I was wondering why you left so soon, what happened?" Emanuel said in an overly eager tone.

"I thought you were so over this?" I said, reminding Emanuel about his intolerance when it came to my drama-filled past.

"I was until you dropped this little piece of info on me. Now you have a real reason to be worried, child."

"Tell me about it," I said, and I felt my stress level jump a few more octaves.

"How do you know for sure it's Todd's?" Emanuel asked.

"I don't, but I'm sure Todd will ask Kai for a paternity test just like he did with me. I have to act as if this baby is his, because if the test comes back positive, I will have a plan ready to go."

"Oooh, what plan is this, if I may be so nosy?" Emanuel asked with an eager tone in his voice.

"Not sure yet, still thinking about it," I said. That was a lie. I knew exactly what I needed to do, I just wasn't ready to share it with Emanuel. "I'm sure you can understand that I need to focus on this for a minute."

"Yeah," he continued, "but don't forget about your career, you're hot right now and you don't want to get cold."

"I know, I know. Listen, let's talk tomorrow about the new role, because I am excited about it despite what's going on in my life right now," I emphasized.

"OK, sounds good. Ciao!"

I hung up my phone and less than two seconds later it rang again. I looked down to see it was Jessica calling. Ugh! I sent her straight to voicemail. I didn't have time for her drama right now. She had been calling non-stop ever since I told her to get over it and move on. But just like a guy she continued to throw

that fishing reel out to see just how much she could
pull back in.

I checked my watch. I had a good half-hour
before I had to be at my shoot, so I decided to drop by
Todd's office since it was on the way. If he refused to
pick up my calls then he was forcing me to do what I
do best, make a surprise visit. Besides, it was time to
start implementing my plan of action. I was going to
ask Todd to marry me—well, not that exact day in his
office, but in the next few days after.

I figured I could swing by his office and drop a
few feelers out there and then hit him with the
proposal when he was more relaxed. After Kai gave
us the oh-so-grand news about her baby-to-be, I
thought I should throw the whole getting pregnant
thing on the back burner for a while. Besides, I
thought we should do it the right way, the traditional
way. You know, marriage first and then a baby.

***

I arrived at Todd's office a little past one and
noticed that it was pretty empty. Todd's secretary
informed me that he was out to lunch with a client
and wouldn't be back until around 3:30pm. I tried his
cell phone again but it went straight to voicemail,
which only annoyed me even more, so I headed into
his office to leave him a memo on his desk. I was just
about done when I looked up to see Maceo standing
in the doorway staring at me, as if I were his prey.

I never cared for Maceo and told Todd that numerous times, but he blew it off like I was the crazy one. Maceo reminded me of a slick rat, just waiting for the perfect opportunity to be devious, and this time was no different. I tried to ignore him in hopes that he would just walk away but he slowly made his way into Todd's office, despite my strong body language that screamed, Don't even think about it!

"So what brings you to Daniels and Smith?" Maceo asked as he gave me a slick-ass smile and rubbed his slick ass hands together.

"I'm hear to see Todd, so if you don't mind..."

"Oh, I don't mind at all, not one bit," Maceo said as he continued to walk toward me, finally taking a seat across from me at Todd's desk. I stop writing and finally gave his ass some eye contact.

"What can I do you for, Maceo?" I asked, digging deep to find my extra-polite voice.

"Nothing, I just saw you saunter in and wanted to come say hello."

"Well, hello," I said, and goodbye, I thought as I focused back on my note, hoping he would get the hint and leave.

"Have I told you how fine you are?" Maceo asked as he looked me up and down, damn near licking his lips.

"Thank you, but no need for the compliments, I already have a man for that." I said. I hurried to finish up my memo to Todd so I could get out of the Maceo snake pit as soon as possible.

"Right, right, your man. How is that going by the way, you and Todd—and Kai?"

I look up to see a devious look on Maceo's face. Clearly Todd had filled him in on what was going on in our lives, which pissed me off to no end.

"We are fine and none of your business, by the way," I said as I finished my letter and stood to leave. Maceo stood up as well. I walked from behind the desk and headed for the door.

"Damn, that ass is looking right," Maceo said when I was two feet from the door. I turned around to look at him.

"Yes, it is, and if you ever touch it, I will break your face," I said with a polite smile.

"Is that right? Well, you may just like it."

I ignored Maceo's comment and turned to walk out when he grabbed my arm. "You know, you really need to be with a real man, not a popcorn version like what you're fucking with."

I looked down at Maceo's grip on my forearm and pulled away.

"Go to hell. For the record, I wouldn't fuck you with a diseased pussy," I said as I headed out the door.

"Jackass," I said loud enough for him to hear before turning the corner outside of Todd's office.

I heard Maceo laugh and say something as I headed down the hallway, but I couldn't make it out since I had already tuned him out. I jumped on the elevator and as the doors closed I took a deep breath. I couldn't understand why Todd kept him around. The last time I told Todd about Maceo's behavior toward me, Todd just brushed it off like I was making the shit up. I didn't need that right then, I just needed to get home and wait for Todd.I also needed a damn drink.

Chapter 34
TODD

I arrived home from the office around 9:30pm hoping Alana would be asleep. She usually went to bed pretty early and I was banking on a quiet evening alone. But when I walked in the house and saw Alana sitting on the couch drinking a glass of wine I knew that plan was going nowhere. I had been avoiding Alana since "that night" with Kai. I knew Alana and I needed to talk about it, but I wasn't ready, at least not until I got things straight with Kai.

"Hey," I said as I put down my briefcase, closing the front door behind me.

""Hey, baby," Alana said as she gave me a small smile. "Did you get my message at work today?"

"I did, I didn't have much time to call you back, I, um…" I mumbled.

"Todd, I know you've been avoiding me and that's fine, but eventually we do have to talk about this," Alana said, cutting me off then taking a short sip of her red wine.

I was a little surprised to hear that come out of Alana's mouth.

I sat down next to Alana and she turned her body toward me on the couch. "How are you?" she asked.

"Good, just a bit overtaxed is all."

"Yeah, me too," she said.

There was an awkward moment of silence, and then she resumed.

"Todd, I've been thinking, maybe after all this blows over we should start making some marriage plans."

I couldn't believe Alana would even bring something like this up, especially now.

"Marriage plans?" I repeated, thinking, where is this coming from? "Alana, let's just take one step at a time, OK? This is not the time to be talking about marriage, seriously."

"I know," she replied, "that's why I said 'after this blows over' and I know you have to do the whole paternity thing with Kai and all. I mean you do plan on doing that, right?" Alana asked as she looked away then back at me. Alana's comment and sidebar question triggered something that Maceo had mentioned when I told him everything that had gone down, about how I should get another paternity test done on Riley. I figured I should give Alana the benefit of the doubt and just ask to see the original test report.

"Yeah, I, um, I plan on doing that," I said.

"Good. I was hoping so, because you want to be 100% sure, right?" Alana asked.

"Yeah, of course. I know we took one when it came to Riley, but you never gave me the original. I'm going to need that," I said, looking at Alana. She turned to me with a scowl on her face.

"Why? Don't you believe me?"

"Yeah," I said. "I just need to see the original document, not a photocopy like you gave me, that's all."

"Unbelievable," Alana murmured.

"Alana, why are tripping on that, for God's sake, I am a lawyer and if a client gives me a copy of something that's important I always ask for the original."

"So now you're treating me like a client?" Alana asked. "Real nice, Todd."

"Alana, I don't want to start a fight, really," I said, hoping she would just calm down.

Alana took another sip of her wine. "Fine," she said, "but I have to look for it, it's been a while since I've seen it."

"OK, whenever you can get it to me. I'm going to go take a shower and head to bed, I'm pretty beat," I said as I stood, thinking I should grab a glass of wine myself to unwind.

Alana put her glass down on the table as she looked up at me and said, "Why don't I join you, in that shower, that is," with a seductive grin.

"Actually, I'm just going to take a quick one if you don't mind," I said as I leaned down and gave her a peck on the forehead before heading upstairs. I knew Alana was trying, but right at that moment I just needed my space.

If she's smart, I thought, she'd give it to me.

***

I woke up and looked at the clock, it was 11:35pm. I must have drifted off to sleep on the couch. The last thing I remembered was hearing Todd turn on the shower upstairs. Todd was pulling away from me and I needed to figure out a way to reel him back in. I thought the marriage thing would be a start, but clearly that had backfired.

I sat in the silence of our living room and nothing came to mind until my phone rang. It was Jessica calling me. I didn't want to pick up but I knew if I kept blowing her off she would just get even more pissed and relentless, not to mention I might be able to use her one last time.

"Hey, you," I said as I answered the phone.

"You know what Kai, you are really a piece of work. I just called to tell you—"

"I miss you and I'm sorry for blowing you off," I quickly interrupted, before Jessica could cuss me out and totally blow me off, once and for all. I needed to keep her around.

"You're so full of shit," Jessica said as I felt her seething through the phone.

"No, really, I want to apologize. I've just had a lot going on. Maybe we could start over," I said, hoping my sentiment didn't come off as fake.

"What do you want, Alana?"

"Nothing, really, I just, I've just been an asshole and wanted to apologize, that's all."

Jessica was silent for a few seconds before she spoke again. I thought for a minute that she had hung up the phone.

"Well, thanks for the apology, it means a lot. And for the record, I've missed the hell out of you too."

she said her voice much softer than it had been when I had picked up.

"I know," I said in a playful way, and we both got a laugh out of that.

"So what's all this that you have going on in your life?" Jessica inquired.

I took a deep breath and lay back down on the couch. "It's way too much to get into right now, but long story short, I'm having some issues with my man."

"Really?"

"Yeah, and we're just trying to take one day at a time and work it out."

"Well, that's a relationship for you," Jessica said.

"Tell me about it."

"Is there anything I can do to help?" she asked.

A broad smile escaped across my face and, once again, Jessica fell right into my plan of action. "You know, it's so funny that you would ask that because just the other day my man brought you up."

"Really, why?"

"He, um, he asked what was up with the woman I met a few months back in the restaurant."

"Why would he ask about me?" Jessica inquired.

"He was hinting around for a threesome."

"A threesome? I thought you said I wasn't his type," she said.

Damn, this bitch has a good memory, I thought. I needed to think quickly. "Girl, he was just talking. He just doesn't like to share sometimes."

"I can understand that. I don't want to share you either," Jessica said laughing.

"Sooo, would you be down for a threesome with me and my man?" I asked, holding my breath and hoping Jessica wouldn't turn me down. I needed this to help bring Todd back in a bit. Jessica was quiet on the other end, a little too quiet, but I held my ground and didn't say a word.

"What about this?" Jessica said, breaking the silence. "You come over tomorrow and I'll have you to myself and then I'll do the threesome with you and your man."

This woman always had a damn agenda. But I needed to do it. It could bring Todd back since he had always wanted a threesome. I realized it was a long shot doing it with a woman he wasn't feeling 100% about, but then again, why bring a Beyoncé lookalike into your bedroom? That wouldn't be a very smart move.

"What time should I be at your apartment?" I asked, rolling my eyes, thinking, here we go again.

"Tomorrow night at 9 works for me, beautiful."

"I'll see you then," I said before hanging up the phone, then grabbing the blanket out of my brown leather ottoman. Todd probably wanted his alone time so I threw my blanket over myself and made the couch my bed for the rest of the night.

Chapter 35
KAI

Toni was definitely a godsend as she sat next to me in my very first Lamaze class. I wasn't prepared to do this alone and I was just happy Toni was open enough and willing to help me out along the way. I hadn't talked to Todd since we'd met for lunch and honestly, I didn't really expect to. I was sure he had his hands full with the news and, of course, Alana. Plus, I was not one to pressure anyone about anything.

"You ready for this?" Toni said as she shot me a warm smile.

"The class or this baby?" I said making sure we were on the same track.

"The class, of course. The baby is coming whether you're ready or not."

"Yeah, you're so right," I said as I nodded my head in agreement. I closed my eyes and took a few deep cleansing breaths as we waited for the Lamaze teacher to enter. There were about 20 couples in the class, everyone paired up man to woman except Toni and me. Being the only same-gender couple didn't really bother me at all. I think being there alone would have been more embarrassing than anything.

I heard my phone go off in my bag and noticed I had a text message from Todd. It read: Hey Kai, did you have a chance to get those results for me? Hope all is well with you. I kind of rolled my eyes and sighed after reading his text. I mean, come on, he knew damn well this baby was his, but, I would play by his rules.

"Is everything OK?" Toni asked. She had probably seen the disdain on my face as I read the message from Todd.

"Yeah, I'm fine, Todd just texted me, reminding me to get that paternity test done as soon as possible. I don't know why that is so annoying to me."

"Oh, just humor him. Besides, a test is a test and if it comes back that he is the father then he can't come with any excuses, right?"

"Yeah, you're right," I said. "Although it is so his and I know he knows that."

"He's a guy, they all have that 10% hope that it's not, even if they do care. No one likes change and a baby is a big one." Toni said as she shrugged her shoulders. "If you need me to go with you, I will," she added.

"Thanks, I may take you up on that," I said as I noticed our teacher making her way into the room. I quickly texted Todd back and let him know that I would have the results to him by the next week at the latest. I then turned my phone on "vibrate only" and threw it back in my gym bag. The teacher was settling in the front and class was about to begin. Toni slid behind me as instructed and we began with a few breathing exercises as she placed her hands on my stomach. Like I said, Toni was definitely a godsend as I reached around and placed my hands on top of hers, hopefully letting here know that she was appreciated.

Chapter 36
ALANA

I finally got Todd to meet me for a drink. I told him this whole "distance act" needed to stop and we needed to start moving forward with our relationship, so he agreed to meet me for drinks at Koi on Ontario. What I didn't tell Todd was that I had a special surprise for him, something he had been wanting for a long, long time. I arrived at Koi about 20 minutes earlier than our scheduled time just to make sure we got good seats at the bar, an area where we wouldn't be pushed or bumped by other patrons trying to get their martini refills.

It was a Thursday night so I knew Koi would fill up relatively fast. I decided to wear a vintage brown skirt that stopped right above my knees and a pink, fitted tank that I accessorized with three slim, long, gold necklaces and matching bangles, eight to be precise. I washed and air-dried my hair using Todd's favorite hair gel that he loved the smell of.

Yep, I was ready for my next move.

Todd finally arrived about ten minutes past eight and I flagged him down as he walked into the restaurant. My heart started to beat a bit faster in anticipation of the night, so I took another sip of my pomegranate martini and stood to give my man a big hug and a kiss—as well as a view of what I was working with tonight.

"Hey, baby, thanks for coming," I said as we both settled into our bar seats. "I ordered you a beer to start with," I said as I slid the glass toward him.

Todd looked a bit uncomfortable as he adjusted himself in his seat. "This place gets really crowded on Thursdays, I see. What made you pick here?" Todd asked as he took a sip of his beer. I rolled my eyes and looked away, then back at Todd. I couldn't believe he was complaining already. But I wasn't going to let that ruin what I had planned.

"I don't know, baby, it was the first thing that popped into my head. You look very handsome tonight," I said as I ran my hand on his thigh. Todd was wearing a black pinstriped suite, white shirt and cobalt blue tie. He always looked so fresh and clean.

"How was work today, busy?" I continued, trying to lighten the mood a bit, as Todd really needed to loosen up.

"Yeah, but it was a good day," Todd said as he shot me a look, then a longer one.

"You look good tonight," Todd said, finally giving me a compliment. Finally, I thought, what a girl must do to make her man stand up and take notice?

"Thank you, and did you notice, I'm wearing your favorite-smelling hair gel?" I asked as I leaned in close so Todd could get a good whiff of my hair.

"MmmHmm, smells good," Todd said with a smile as I rubbed his leg a bit more.

I took another sip from my martini. "I miss you, baby, I miss us," I said as I leaned in closer to whisper to him. "I miss our lovemaking. I miss our morning time where we have our pillow talk," I continued as I glided my hand over his manhood. Todd took another swig of his beer. "I miss you, too, it's just this thing with Kai threw me off, that's all," Todd said, finally breaking down and talking about his true feelings.

"I know, baby, but I'm here for you. Remember, we're a team, you're my best friend and my lover and we can get through this together, whatever the outcome," I said, emphasizing the whole "together" part, making Todd aware that we were a team and that no one could penetrate that.

Todd took a deep breath and rubbed his face with his right hand. "I know, baby, this is just a lot to handle right now."

"I know it is, but together we can pull through this, OK?" I said. Todd didn't respond but took another swig of his beer. "OK, baby?" I asked again.

"Of course," Todd said, finally giving me a little positive feedback.

I knew it was time to make my move.

"Well, let me help you relax and take your mind off of all of this for a while," I said as I continued to caress his inner thigh. Todd ordered another drink, this time a shot of Patron.

"What do you suggest?" Todd asked, looking down at my hand on his thigh.

I smiled a devious smile and leaned into him. "How about a threesome, baby? I know you've never had one and I want to be the first to give it to you."

"A threesome?" he repeated.

"Yep, with all the bells and whistles," I said with a smile.

Todd was quiet for a minute. He was always such a thinker, always processing shit. "When?" He hesitantly inquired.

"How about tonight?"

"Tonight?" He was repeating everything I said.

"No better time than the present, I say," I said with a flirtatious tone in my voice.

"We don't have a girl, or do we?" he asked.

"I have a girl for us."

"Really? Who?"

I knew I had to be delicate in jogging Todd's memory about Jessica since he had not been an immediate fan of hers when he'd seen her in that restaurant.

"Well, remember the woman from the restaurant a while back, the woman sitting near the back of the restaurant?" I asked.

"I think I do, but was she attractive? I don't remember her being all that attractive."

"No, she is, baby," I assured him.

"I don't know, Kai, I can't remember how she looks and that's usually not a good sign. Maybe we should pick someone else, maybe someone that's here tonight."

"Here? Baby, this isn't a brothel where we can come in and pick some random girl to go home with us. I mean, these days you have to be careful, you know?"

"Yeah, I guess," he said.

"Listen, Jessica is cute and she's safe, too."

"How do you know?" Todd inquired.

"Just trust me, baby, "I said with an assurance in my voice.

"So this Jessica woman, where is she?" Todd asked, looking around the restaurant as if she were lurking in the back somewhere.

"She's not here but I can call her and she can meet us a little later."

"At our house?" Todd asked with a tone of uncertainty.

"No, baby, we can get a hotel room, and keep it all on neutral ground."

Todd was now on his third shot of Patron and by his body language I could tell he was slowly being swayed to do the deed. I decided to call Jessica and tell her to meet us in thirty minutes before his high, as well as his liquid courage, wore off.

"Let me call Jessica and tell her to meet us at the Radisson Suites in like thirty," I said to Todd, making sure he was still down for it.

Todd looked at me then smiled. "That's fine, yeah."

I began to rub his inner thigh again. "Baby, this will be fun, and I will make sure you remember it for a long, long time," I said, as I leaned in and planted a soft seductive kiss on his lips.

After a few more drinks Todd and I left Koi and headed over to the Radisson. Jessica texted me to say that she already had the room and just to come up when we arrived. Todd was a little nervous so I assured him that it was going to be fine and he should just relax and go with the flow.

We entered the hotel and went up the elevator and down the hallway to room 515. I knocked on the door softly and waited for Jessica to let us in. I turned to look at Todd, who had a smile on his face. The alcohol must have worked its way through his bloodstream because he seemed a bit more relaxed. Jessica opened the door with a huge smile on her face. She was already in a sexy outfit, holding a drink in her hand, a bit dramatic but, hey, that was how she rolled.

"Hey, you two, welcome, please come in," Jessica said as she stepped to the side to let Todd and I enter the hotel room. We went in and I noticed right away that she'd booked a suite. I didn't remember agreeing on a suite but it was nice as hell so I wasn't complaining.

"Jessica, this is my man Todd. Todd this is Jessica," I said.

They looked at each other and said their hellos. There was a bit of awkwardness in the air and I knew that we needed to keep the drinks flowing.

"How about I get you two a few cocktails," Jessica said, reading my mind. Todd turned and sat down on the couch as Jessica gave me a wink and headed to the bar.

"You OK, baby?" I asked Todd as I sat down next to him on the couch.

"Yeah, yeah, just you know, just taking this all in. I'm good though, really."

"Good, because I'm excited about tonight," I said, hoping my enthusiasm would rub off on him.

Todd looked over to Jessica who was by the bar. "So that's the same woman that was flirting with you at the restaurant that night, the one that followed you into the bathroom?"

"Yeah, why?"

"I don't know," Todd said, "she looks different than I remember."

"A 'good' different or 'bad' different?"

"Actually she looks better than what I remember," Todd said as he continued to stare at Jessica, mainly her ass.

"See? I told you she wasn't bad looking," I said as Todd continued to give Jessica the once-over.

"So how does this work, this whole threesome thing?" Todd asked.

"What do you mean?"

"Am I supposed to have sex with her? Or do I just watch you two?"

I smiled at Todd's naïve nature when it came to group sex and I was glad he asked, because then I could tell him what I wanted.

***

I woke up and noticed it was 5am. I rolled over to see that Todd was still sound asleep. I sat up and rubbed my face and hair and noticed that Jessica was gone. I slowly slid out the bed to search the suite, just to make sure she hadn't moved to the living room, but there was no sign of her at all. I slid back into the bed next to Todd and my body movement woke him up.

"Hey, you," Todd said as he smiled at me. I pulled in closer to him as we spooned.

"So did you have fun last night?" I asked as I caressed his face, pressing my lips against his. His breath was stale but it didn't bother me one bit.

"I did, thanks for that, it was a nice surprise."

"Yeah, I though you would like it," I said as I kissed Todd's lips then his cheek.

"So your girl was cool, too, we should keep her in our Rolodex for future reference."

I smiled at Todd's willingness to go there again. "Really? OK, I will."

"What time is it?" Todd asked as he lifted his head to sneak a peek at the clock.

"It's a little after 5," I said as he squinted at the clock. "You got time, baby, just relax, you're always rushing off to work."

"Yeah, you're right," Todd said as he lay his head back down and pulled me in closer.

"I miss this, us just cuddling in the bed after a great night of lovemaking," I said.

"Yeah, it feels good," Todd agreed.

I watched him as he closed his eyes and thought that maybe it would be a good time to bring up the marriage thing again.

"Baby?"

"Hmm?"

"Just think, this could easily be us in our honeymoon suite," I said as I kissed Todd's lips again, this time separating them with my tongue. His eyes remained closed. He pulled his head away.

"Alana, I told you, I don't want to talk about the marriage thing yet, not now."

"Then when, Todd?" I asked as irritation escaped my mouth uncontrollably.

Todd opened his eyes. He sighed. "We had a great night last night. Why do you have to ruin it by talking about marriage?"

"Well, I didn't think that talking about our future together would be such a damn downer, Todd."

Todd looked at me, sat up and rubbed his head with his hands.

"I am not going there with you, Alana, not this morning," he said as he stood and started putting on his clothes.

"Then when?" I asked again.

Todd ignored me as he finished dressing and grabbed his coat.

"I'm going to shower back at the condo, I'll see you later."

"Fine."

Todd headed for the door and right before he opened it to walk out, he turned to me. "Drop off those paternity papers at my office today, please, the originals," he said emphatically before heading out the door and closing it behind him.

"Jackass," I said hoping he heard me through the closed door.

I shook my head and flopped back down in the bed. Fucking men.

***

After Maceo and I returned from a late lunch meeting, I entered my office and noticed an envelope on my desk. I opened it to see the paternity test results from Alana. I looked over the paper but then noticed it was another photocopy. The first thing I thought was how clear I had made it to Alana that I wanted the original.

Maceo stepped into my office and noticed me looking at the paper. I tossed it on the desk and picked up my phone to call Alana. Of course, I got her voicemail, which didn't surprise me one bit, based on the morning we'd just had.

"Hey, Alana, it's Todd. I'm looking at the paternity test you dropped off and I noticed it's another copy, I thought I made it clear that I wanted to see the original. Please call me back."

By now Maceo had taken a seat on the couch on the other side of my office, and he began cleaning his fingernails with a small emery board.

"Yo, you asked Alana for the paternity test?" Maceo asked.

"Yeah, I figured I would give her the benefit of the doubt, but you see where that got me."

"I told you man," he said, "asking her would only raise a red flag, now she drops another copy on you and who knows where that original piece of paper work is." Maceo looked up from his nails. "If you ask me, I think she's hiding something."

"Yeah," I replied, "that did cross my mind. Not to mention she's been pressing me lately about getting married."

"Yeah, see, that right there would make me nervous as hell. Your girl is definitely hiding something. You need to get to the bottom of this shit, quick," Maceo said as he went back to cleaning his nails.

"Yeah, no kidding."

"Who's the guy she was married to again?" Maceo asked.

"Ex-Bears cornerback, Avery Anderson," I said.

"The cat that's in jail now for illegal dog fighting, right?" Maceo asked.

"Yeah," I replied, "that's him."

"Yeah, if you ask me, there are way too many red flags on the field not to call a serious time out on her ass."

"Tell me about it," I said, agreeing with Maceo.

"I can do some snooping around if you want. I got a few boys in the NFL."

I sat down at my desk and for the first time, something didn't feel right about Alana and my connection to Riley. But why would she lie to me about me being the father to her child? I wondered. I knew it was time to get to the bottom of that mess once and for all.

"Yeah, a little snooping may be exactly what the doctor ordered."

Chapter 37

KAI

Although Toni and I were growing closer it was still nice to have my best friend Simone in town for the weekend. She flew up the day before to help throw together my mini baby shower, which would probably consist of her, my mom and my sister—and, of course, a few random people I'd met along the way in New York. But that was fine with me, I was happy to have some familiar faces around for a while.

Simone and I settled down on my couch as we sipped on raspberry fusion tea from Starbucks and snacked on Townhouse cookies. These were the moments that I wished me and Simone still lived in the same city. I always felt so relaxed around my best friend and she definitely knew how to make herself comfortable in my space. We could sit around all day and just lounge and talk and it would all be oh so fulfilling.

"So how is it going with you and Todd?" Simone asked as she continued to sip from her oversized teacup. She was curled up in my loveseat and wrapped in one of my throw-covers.

"Well, it's going, I had my doctor mail him the original results of the paternity test, so I guess he should have either gotten it by now or will soon."

"I can't believe his ass even asked for one," Simone said. "He knows that baby is his."

"Yeah," I said, "but Todd is so calculating, you know that, and he is never one to assume anything. He needs proof and evidence to back up everything."

"I guess," Simone said. "I wonder how that relationship is going with Alana, like I really care."

I stretched a bit, letting out a big yawn, and said, "According to Todd, they are taking it one day at a time."

"Hmm, code for 'I'm miserable but I can't let you know that.'"

"Do you think they will get married?" I asked, trying not to sound like I cared. Deep down inside, though, I did.

"For his sake, I hope not. That bitch is crazy, you know, and I cannot understand for the life of me how he does not see that. Hell, maybe her pussy is lined in platinum and sprinkled in gold, but then again, you would probably know that, right?" Simone said with a chuckle.

"Oh, shut it," I said with a smile. My days with Alana seemed so far away, almost as if they had never even happened, but the moment I looked down at my stomach and remembered that it was just me and the baby now, I was quickly reminded that it did happen, indeed.

"So what did you think of Toni?" I asked Simone, knowing she would give me her honest opinion.

"She seems nice. You two have been friends ever since you've moved here, right?"

"The very first day. She's been a real godsend."

"Yeah, I can see that about her, she seems very, um, nurturing, although there is something about her that I couldn't quite put my finger on."

"Wait a minute. You, Simone McCormick, can always peg someone the moment you meet them."

"I know, shocking isn't it? But, no, I'm missing something with her. One thing I did pick up on was that she is very protective of you."

"Really? I never noticed that." I said.

"Of course you wouldn't, for the main reason that when you two are together it's just you two," Simone said. "But nonetheless, it's good to have a support system, no matter how small it is."

"Yeah, she is great and she really is someone that has helped me through some hard times."

"I'm not saying she isn't great, but remember, you haven't known her for years and you definitely don't know everything about her, so just keep your eyes open."

"Yes, mom," I replied.

Simone and I stayed on my couch most of the day. I needed that time with my best friend and I knew the feeling was mutual.

Chapter 38
TODD

I left work early in an attempt to beat Alana home. Maceo had made a good point: If she is not giving me the original paternity test, what is she hiding? I entered the condo and noticed that no one was home. It was 4:15pm on a Friday afternoon and I remembered Alana saying she and Riley had a play date after school, so I had a little time to do some snooping.

Alana had a desk in the kitchen that she used from time to time, and I noticed that she kept the top drawer locked. I headed over to the desk and sat down and quickly confirmed that the drawer was, in fact, locked. I felt under and behind the desk for a key, and then looked around for anything that I could use to unlock the drawer, but found nothing. For some odd reason I needed to get in that drawer. So I grabbed a sharp knife but, of course, it didn't fit.

Dammit.

I glanced at my watch and noticed that 20 minutes had already gone by. Suddenly, I had a thought. Most desk drawer keys were not that unique and I wondered if my own desk key would somehow work on hers. Hell, it was worth a try.

I went to my office and grabbed the key out of its secret hiding place and brought it back over to Alana's kitchen desk. I inserted it and voilà, it worked like a charm. The first thing I noticed was that Alana's desk drawer was filled to the top with tons of paperwork from Victoria's Secret all the way back to her first modeling job with Kai. She really needs a filing cabinet, I thought.

I started digging through the mounds of paper, unfolding, folding and placing the unnecessary items to one side, trying to keep in mind the order in which I pulled them out so I could put them back without her noticing that they'd been tampered with. Then I came across a piece of paper that matched my photocopy with Genetic Technologies, Inc., across the top. That's what I was searching for and no surprise, it was the original.

I pulled out my copy from my briefcase and began to compare the two. The first page was identical, but when I got to the second page I saw a huge discrepancy. The line entitled "Probability of Paternity" did not read the same as it did on my copy. On Alana's original copy the probability figure was 33% and right under that it read:

Based on results from the nine genetic systems listed above Todd Daniels can be excluded as the biological father of Riley Brooks as determined by the presence of the obligate paternal allele of all of these systems.

The rest of the original second page was the same as my copy.

I sat back upon reading this. Riley isn't my child? What the hell is going on? At that moment, I didn't care that I had gone through Alana's belongings and broken into her desk, because right then I was pissed the fuck off.

I recalled my conversation with Kai, less than eight months before, when we met for lunch and how she kept trying to get me to see that I could not trust Alana. "She will use you just like she uses everyone else," were Kai's exact words. A familiar feeling fell over me, the same feeling I felt the day I found out Kai was sleeping with Alana behind my back, a feeling of utter betrayal. I began to breathe erratically and suddenly, I wanted to punch something hard, very hard. Why would Alana lie about Riley?

"Fuck!" I yelled, only to look up and see Riley and Alana standing not 10 feet away.

I locked eyes with Alana and noticed a look of fear on her face, and I knew why.

"Riley, sweetie, go to your room," I said without taking my eyes off of Alana.

As Riley turned and ran upstairs I grabbed the two documents from the mess on Alana's desk and stood up.

"I'm giving you one chance to come clean," I said as I took two steps toward her.

Alana did not move. She didn't take one step. "One… one chance to come clean about what?" Alana stuttered.

I laughed, looking down at the documents and laying them side-by-side on the counter. "About this, Alana." I put them in clear sight and just took a step back and folded my arms. "I think you know what."

Alana never looked down at the papers. She didn't have to. She knew exactly what time it was.

"I just want to know why? Why did you lie?"

"I didn't want to lose you and I knew how much Riley loved you and…"

I cut her off. "Stop bullshitting me, Alana! Why did you lie?" I demanded again, this time loud enough hopefully to pull it out of her.

"I… um… I don't know."

"Really, you don't know, huh? Well how about this," I said, "I'm moving out so you can have all the time alone to figure it out."

I grabbed the original paternity report and walked past Alana as she stood in the same spot she'd landed on when she walked in the kitchen. Alana grabbed my left arm and I forcefully jerked it away. "Don't fucking touch me," I said as I keep it moving. I was just about at the stairs when she called out.

"So you're just going to abandon me and your daughter, just like that? What kind of man just walks out on his family?'

"The kind that's been lied to for the last 6 months, that's what kind." I turned back from the stairs and said, "You know, I think I'll just come back for my things later."

I headed towards the front door but before leaving I looked Alana dead in her eyes, "You better pray, I don't try to take Riley away from you, because you are clearly not stable."

I walked out the door, closing it tightly behind me. I stood on the porch and breathed in the evening air. I wasn't sure where I was going, but I knew it wasn't back into my condo or into Alana's web of lies.

***

I felt numb, as if I were waking from a bad dream, but I knew it was not a dream at all. I heard Todd drive away and I knew in my heart of hearts he was not coming back, not even for Riley's sake. How could I have been so stupid to keep that document in the house? I should have shredded it when I had the chance, I thought. I felt the pieces of my life starting to unravel and I needed to figure out how to put them back together before it was too late. Finding that piece to connect with Todd would be the biggest challenge of my life, but I had to figure something out, I simply could not, no, would not let that be the end of us. I sat down at my desk and started putting my papers back into the drawer when my cell phone rang. Without looking at the display I picked up, it hoping it was Todd.

"Todd?" I asked with an enthusiastic tone.

"No, baby, it's me, Jessica."

"Jessica, I can't talk."

"What's wrong now? No, let me guess—more drama in your life."

I felt my stomach turn. I was so not in the mood for her. "Yeah, I gotta go."

"You're going to get enough of playing hard to get, you know you want this," Jessica said with total flirtation in her voice.

I laughed. "You just don't get it do you?" I said irritated to the nth degree, mostly from what had just gone down with Todd, although Jessica was doing a good job of her own. This woman had picked the wrong fucking time to call me.

"I don't get what, Alana?" Jessica asked.

"That I don't want you, never have."

"Excuse me?" Jessica protested.

"You were nothing but a ploy in my master plan and now your services are no longer needed. So take the fucking hint and fuck off! Or if that's too much for your feeble brain, I'll translate it for you! Lose my number!" I said with a full load of venom in my voice. I threw my cell phone across the room and swept the papers off my desk onto the floor and cried like I had never cried before.

Chapter 39
TODD

I jumped in my car after leaving Alana with her thoughts and I headed to Nicco's on Dearborn, mostly because it was the closest bar I could think of at the time. I didn't know what to do or whom to talk to. All I knew was that I felt very used. I'd been burned many times before by women, but this time Alana managed to take the world championship.

Nicco's was relatively empty and that was just fine with me since I was in no mood to talk to anyone. I was on my second vodka on the rocks by the time Maceo came strolling in. He had called as I was leaving my condo and I had given him the quick version of what had gone down with Alana. He mentioned that he had some info to share with me, as well as give me a document that came to the office from Kai after I'd left. I told him where I was headed, and he said he would be over in twenty minutes. My head was spinning as I downed my third drink and realized that I needed to pull back a little.

"Sup, bro?" Maceo asked as he slid into the bar stool next to mine.

"Too much, man," I said. "So what do you have for me?" I asked as I looked at him.

Maceo slid a business size envelope to me on the bar as he flagged down the bartender and ordered a few shots of Patron. I grabbed the envelope and opened it, noticing the familiar logo of the genetic testing company. It was Kai's paternity results and I was not surprised in the least that it said, right there in black and white, that the chance of me being the father of her child was 99.99%. I took a deep breath and laid the letter back down on the bar. Maceo picked it up and read what I had just digested.

"Damn!" Maceo said, looking at me trying to read my body language.

"Yeah, damn is right," I said, mirroring Maceo's reaction.

Maceo turned and took both of his shots of tequila back to back, then turned back toward me.

"Well, if it's any consolation, congrats."

"Yeah, thanks," I replied.

"As far as Alana, that's fucked up, but are you really that surprised?"

"Right now, nothing can surprise me much," I said as Maceo flagged down the bartender and ordered yet another shot.

"Can I get you one?" Maceo asked.

"Thanks, but I'm good."

"Listen, I have some other news for you, regarding Alana."

"I'm listening," I said as I looked straight ahead, sipping on my vodka.

"I talked to my boy about her ex, Avery Anderson, and get this, that cat was flat broke when he went to jail. Most of his shit was liquidated when he got caught up and everything that wasn't, was sucked up by his lawyer. Bottom line, his ass is flat broke. No wonder Alana lied and said you were the baby's daddy; she needed a second income, yo. Avery didn't have the funds anymore and probably never will. When he gets released he will be lucky to get a job flippin' burgers."

I took another deep breath and then waved the bartender down to order that shot of Patron.

"It all makes sense now. How fucking stupid could I have been, man?" I said. I felt as if my life was crashing down all around me. "Kai was right the whole time. Alana set all this up from the beginning."

"Listen, don't beat yourself up," Maceo said, "bitches will always try to get us and sometimes a few of them succeed."

I just rubbed my head. I couldn't believe I'd let myself fall this deep.

I looked again at Kai's letter sitting on the bar. "I should have never taken Alana's word over Kai's," I muttered to myself before turning to Maceo. "I should be with Kai, I never should have left her."

"Then go to New York, tell her you fucked up."

"Yeah, right. It's too late for that," I said.

"Yo, it's never too late if you think she's the one."

"She'll never take me back, not after how I treated her, not after how I took Alana over her."

"Well, technically, she did you wrong first, so in hindsight you two are even now."

I had to laugh at Maceo's thought pattern, but he had a point. "What if she still turns me down?"

"Then walk away and come back with another angle," he said.

"So you want me to beg?"

"Shit, if this is the woman you think you need to be with, then hell, yeah," Maceo said.

I turned to look at Maceo straight in the eyes. "This is advice coming from 'The Maceo Smith,' right?"

"Yo, listen, Kai sounds like a good woman," he said. "I mean, seriously, if I could find one to tame my ass, I would."

"You?" I scoffed.

"Well, she would have to be one hell of woman, but yeah," Maceo insisted.

I had to laugh out loud at that one. "Man," I said, "you are like a bag of tricks, you know that?"

"Anything to keep the bitches on their toes. Gotta keep 'em guessing."

"Apparently so," I said and I took my last shot for the night. "I need to be in New York, like, tomorrow."

"Then why are you sitting here with me? Get your ass to New York," Maceo said. He always knew what I needed to hear, prompting me as he did with his words and body language.

"You're right," I said as I stood. "Thanks."

"And don't worry about the practice," Maceo said. "I'll hold it down until you come back."

"Thanks, man," I said as I scooped Kai's letter off the bar and grabbed my jacket, heading out of Nicco's. I knew I had a big challenge ahead of me, but for some reason I was finally ready to fight for what I wanted. Until that moment, I had never known so clearly what I wanted in my life.

Kai and this baby.

Chapter 40

KAI

It had been a long day at the office and I was running late for my appointment with Dr. Albridge. I was close to delivering this baby and daily activities like bending over or even walking up a flight of stairs had become some of my biggest challenges. My stomach had grown to the size of three basketballs and there were nights when sleep felt like a distant dream of the past. I figured it was just the universe's way of getting me ready for the birth of my son. I wasn't gonna get a lot of sleep when he got here, so I guess my body was training me on how to get through the day on less than four hours of sleep.

I glanced at my watch and noticed it was just past four pm. I knew if I left now I could catch the B train and be back in Brooklyn for my appointment by 5:15.

I stood to gather my things when I noticed my pants were wet. I had on a black maternity dress with my flat sandals so it wasn't like I was hot and experiencing an uncontrollable heat flash. I stepped aside to see that the floor was also wet below me and suddenly I knew that my water had broken. In that moment I froze, knowing I had to get to Brooklyn right away. I grabbed my cell phone and called my doctor who told me to relax and that he would meet me at the hospital as soon as possible. Next, I called Toni and told her I was going into labor, so she could grab my bag and meet me at the hospital.

I headed towards the elevator as I glanced back at my watch; I needed to start timing these contractions. From the time I got out of the building my contractions were twelve minutes apart, lasting around five minutes each.

I jumped in a cab and before I knew it I was pulling up to Brooklyn Memorial Hospital and checking myself in. My contractions were only about

12 minutes apart now so according to my doctor I wasn't near delivery yet.

"So how are you doing?" Dr. Katz asked me as I settled into my hospital bed equipped with that infamous hospital garment. The sound of the monitor that tracked my contractions echoed throughout my room

"I feel OK."

"Good, you are about three centimeters dilated, so I will be back in a few minutes."

"Oh, Dr. Katz, when do you give out the feel good drug?" I smiled.

He smiled back. "Ah, the infamous epidural, I'm assuming you are referring to?"

"That would be the one."

"Let's give it a few more centimeters. Right now you are good. Just stay relaxed and keep doing your breathing exercises."

"OK," I said as he headed out of my hospital room. A few minutes later Toni walked in with my bag over her shoulder.

"Hey, hey, this is it," Toni said as she put my bag down on the chair next to my bed and walked over to my beside. "How are you feeling?"

"Good for now, but I'm sure that won't last," I said in a joking manner, mainly to keep my anxiety to a minimum.

"You will be fine."

"Can you do me a favor and call Simone and my mom?"

"What about Todd?" Toni asked.

"Oh, yes, of course, gotta let the baby's daddy know his child is about to be born. My phone is in my purse over there," I said as I pointed in the direction of the table near the window. Toni took my phone out of my purse and headed out the room to make the calls for me.

My contractions were now 10 minutes apart and I was starting to feel very uncomfortable. I began to breathe as I reached for my iPod to help distract my mind from the pain with some soothing music. I closed my eyes for a few seconds only to open them to see my nurse. I pulled off my headphones as I watched her monitor my contractions.

"I think you are ready for your epidural," the nurse said.

"Oh good. Please bring it." My contractions were starting to get more intense by the minute. My nurse exited the room and minutes later two new faces entered. The two men introduced themselves as the anesthesiologist and a resident. I sat up as instructed as the doctor told me to lean over on a pillow. I felt a small pinch, a little heat entering my back, and then nothing. I was in euphoric heaven. I slowly laid back down on my bed. My contractions now only felt like a little pressure instead of the intense cramps that ricocheted from my back down to my calves and back up again.

***

I must have drifted off for about an hour, because when I woke I noticed it was night time. My nurse was standing over me typing something into the computer that was connected to all my monitors. I was now dilated eight centimeters. Dr. Katz came back in and I looked over wondering where Toni was. Dr. Katz looked at the monitor, and then turned to me, "you ready to push this baby out?" He said as he touched my arm.

"Now?" I said, thinking, I was sooo not ready for this.

"Do you have something else you have to do right now?" Dr. Katz said in his sarcastic tone.

"I guess not, huh?"

"Good, then let's do this."

"O… kay."

I leaned backed and closed my eyes, I couldn't believe I was about to push this baby through, I felt my contractions coming full force and it was very uncomfortable. I wanted this to be over, I wanted to be holding my child, but this was something I couldn't avoid, ready or not, the baby was about to make it's entrance into this world. I took a deep breath as I looked up to see Toni coming back into my room, and to my ultimate surprise, Todd was behind her.

"Look who I ran into in the hallway." Toni said as she smiled at me. I couldn't believe Todd was here, how did he know I was in labor?

"Hey,"

"What are you doing here?"

"I got the paternity results and jumped on the first plane."

"Your timing couldn't have been more perfect," I said and we exchanged a smile. I was way too tired and scared to question Todd's motives, I was just glad he was there.

My nurse came over to me and prepped me for the pushing. I braced my left leg against Todd and the other on my nurse as I barred down and pushed like I had never pushed before. The pain was something that I had never experienced before as well as something I never wanted to go through ever again. But, one hour later, I successfully pushed out my son. He was 7 pounds and 3 ounces of pure beauty. He was perfect as Dr. Katz layed him on my chest, still covered with blood and mucus and all the inside stuff he lived in for the last 9 months, but I didn't care, I was in love.

Chapter 41
ALANA

I was sitting in Kurt's Café waiting for Emanuel.
We'd finally found a time to meet so he could fill me
in on my new film that shoots in New York. I was
pretty excited to hear about the project for the mere
fact that I would be in New York. I definitely needed
something to take my mind off of Todd. It had been a
little over a month since he moved out and so far, it
had been very hard for me as well as Riley.

Emanuel finally came in as if he had just run a
marathon. He was out of breath and very much

windblown. He could be a bit spastic at times. I guess in the gay world they just call it dramatic.

"Sorry I'm late girlfriend. Child, what is up with the traffic in downtown Chicago?"

"I think it's called rush hour, but call me crazy," I said trying to put him in a better mood.

"OK, I don't have a whole lot of time. I'm supposed to be meeting a new client in thirty at the office."

"So why didn't we just meet at your office then?" I asked wondering why Emanuel was killing himself.

"Because I haven't even been there yet today. I just got out the bed three hours ago," Emanuel said with a slight grin on his face, which translated to late night booty call that rolled over to breakfast and lunch in bed. I wasn't going to touch that one.

"So, what's the 411 on my new starring role?" I said as I rubbed my hands together. I felt as if I were about to receive the jewels of the Nile.

"Well, it is a good role, better than the last one for sure."

"OK, I'm listening."

"This time around you will be playing the sister to Victoria Saunders."

I stopped for a minute to think of who the hell this woman was. Emanuel saw my mind working overtime trying to figure out who this woman was.

"Ah, hello, 'A stranger is coming, Marathon Woman'—do you ever go to the movies, child?"

"Oh, right. So I'm playing her sister? Isn't she Colombian?"

"Yes but technically you are her half-sister."

"Well, OK," I said.

"Anyway, child, it starts shooting in two weeks." His tone softened, "How are you with Riley? Will Todd be able to watch her?"

I took a sip of the Evian water sitting in front of me. "Todd and I are still apart, and for the record I really don't want to talk about it right now. But my mom can watch her while I am there. How long is the shoot for?"

Emanuel flipped through his paper work. "Well, your part is only six days."

"Yeah, that is doable, for sure." I said.

Emanuel began to pack up his things. "Sorry, child, but I have to get going. I will email you the itinerary as well as the pay, which, unfortunately, is not the greatest."

"What do you mean not the greatest?"

"Well since this is an Indie project most of the payment is on the back end."

"What?"

"This film will be a hit, I guarantee it, I promise, you'll be a big hit at Sundance.

"Forget it, I pass."

"Pass? You can't pass on this. Besides, I already told the director you would do it."

"Well then tell the director if he wants me, he has to pay me. I'm sure he's paying that Vanessa woman."

"Victoria," Emanuel corrected me.

"Whatever. Being a big hit in Sundance isn't going to pay my mortgage."

"Fine, I will work on it." Emanuel stood and paused for a second, as he put his hands on his hips.

"Alana, keep in mind that sometimes you have to give a little, to get a lot."

"Story of my life Emanuel, just get me a paycheck, k?"

"I hope so, because I cannot do anything for free."

"You are something else," he said before leaning down and giving me a small peck on the cheek.

"Ciao, Bella," I said and reached for my java sitting on the table

"I will call you," Emanuel said as he turned and left, just as fast as he'd come in.

I sipped on my double mocha chai latte and noticed a familiar face enter the café, head up to the counter and place an order. I couldn't tell if I really knew this woman since she had on large dark sunglasses and was showing off her profile from where I was sitting. When she turned around to finally face me I knew exactly whom it was, it was fucking Simone, Kai's best friend. Shit.

I immediately turned my body toward the window in hopes she wouldn't see me, but the moment I did that and looked back over to the front counter, her ass was walking toward me with much purpose.

"Well, well, well, if it isn't Alana Brooks," Simone said as she stopped in front of me with a huge grin on her face. She took a few sips of her coffee. I was so not in the mood for this bitch.

"Simone, right?" I asked, knowing damn well exactly who she was, but why give her that satisfaction? Simone was always hot and cold with me, and it only got worse after the whole Kai/Todd breakup went down.

"Nice try, Alana, but you know good and damn well who I am, or should I remind you that I was the one who jumpstarted this whole makeshift career of yours?"

"Oh, that's right, my bad, how could I have ever forgotten that, especially since you continually remind me every time I see you?"

"Well, you know, the memory is the first thing to go, darlin'," Simone said, removing her sunglasses.

"So," I asked, "what brings you to Kurt's and this pleasant surprise visit from you?"

"McKenzie and Strong is a block down or have you already forgotten your humble beginnings?"

I had to laugh at that bitch; she thought she was so damn grand. "For your information, Simone, my humble beginnings were way before McKenzie and Strong."

"Oh, right, right. Was that before or after you went after a pro football player solely for his money, who cheats on you like it was his job? Wait don't answer that, must've been after. The $5,000 boob job gives it away.

"Did you want something, Simone? Because if not, this conversation is over," I said through my clenched teeth. I would usually be all over a bitch, but I knew nothing about Simone and didn't have any dirt on her at all. How could I have let that shit happen?

"So funny you asked," Simone said as she shifted her stance from her right to her left. "I don't know if you knew but Kai had her baby yesterday."

"Really, well, thanks for that piece of news, but I could really give a shit."

"Yeah, sure ya don't, but I'm sure you will care about Todd being there by her side, seeing that it is his son and all."

"What? Todd is in New York?"

"Oh, yeah, didn't you know?" Simone said with a huge satisfied grin on her face.

I felt my body temperature rise with every syllable that fell from Simone's sarcastic mouth.

"He flew to be by her side. I mean you know how Todd can be when he finds out he has a child and all. Oh, how's Riley by the way? Ya find a new father for her yet?"

"Fuck you, Simone, OK. Riley has one father and that is Todd," I said as I gathered my belongings and headed out the café. I walked a few steps away, grabbed my cell phone and immediately dialed Todd's number but it went directly into voicemail. That was fine, I didn't need to talk to him, because I was headed to New York on the next plane. I informed Emanuel with a text that I would be in New York a week ahead of schedule, so he needed to expedite my pay for the movie. It was time to cut through the bullshit and get my man back.

Chapter 42
TODD

The thought of spending the next 20 years without Kai and Kristopher broke me down. It had only been two days since Kai gave birth to our son and I needed to see them again. The moment I saw my son in the hospital I knew I had made a big, big mistake choosing Alana over Kai, but I had to stop beating myself up about it, it was time to take action. Kai texted me to let me know that she was heading home from the hospital that morning and I realized she probably needed some time to settle in. I figured if I swung by that evening I could give her a helping hand. I left my hotel room, headed to the store to pick up a few of her favorites and took a cab to her apartment in Brooklyn.

I arrived at her doorstep around 6:30 pm and wasn't surprised when I knocked on her door that Toni, her upstairs neighbor, answered.

"Todd, hey, was Kai expecting you?"

"No, but I thought she might need some things so I thought—"

"Hey, no need to come up with excuses to see your son, come in, I'm sure she will be happy to see you."

I smiled at Toni's optimistic attitude; I only hoped Kai shared her enthusiasm about my unexpected visit.

I headed back Kai's bedroom where she was laying in the bed nursing Kristopher.

She looked up as I walk in the room, bags in hand and the right intentions in my heart. "Hey, what are you doing here?" Kai said in a soft voice so as not to interrupt Kristopher as he was drifting off to sleep.

"I, um, I thought you might need some things," I said as I lifted the two bags from the corner store. "I brought your favorites, I mean, that is to say, if they still are your favorites." For some reason, I felt very nervous and apprehensive.

"Ah, thanks and for the record, I will always like my favorites," Kai said with a smile on her face. She looked down at our son. "Look who's here, Kristopher, it's your daddy," Kai said to our son. I just stood there, not really sure of what to do.

"Um, I can go put these away if you like."

"Oh, that can wait, would you like to burp him? He is just about done eating."

"Oh, um, sure, yes," I said. "Although I'm not sure if I know how."

"Oh, it's easy," Kai said as she stood, put a receiving blanket in my arms then put Kristopher on top of that. "Here, take a seat in the rocker and just put him on your shoulder and pat his back."

I followed Kai's orders like a child in obedience school. I held my son close again and a feeling came over me I could not explain. As I rocked and patted and rocked and patted his little back, which wasn't much bigger than the palm of my hand, I focused all my energy on him. Every part of my being was directed at Kristopher and only Kristopher, and it felt so right.

"See, you're a pro," Kai said as she smiled and sat back down on the bed.

"Yeah, I guess," I said, looking up at Kai for a second then right back down at my son.

"Hey," she said, "I will be right back, I'm going to put the groceries away."

As Kai left the bedroom, I stared down at my son, who was drifting in and out of a sleepy state and then finally a cute little burp escaped through his little lips and the smell of sour milk engulfed my senses. After that, I wasn't sure what came next, so I just laid him down in my lap and stared at his precious little face. In that moment, a tear fell from my eye and I knew it was time for me to tell Kai exactly how I felt.

"Hey, looks like he is knocked out," Kai said as she came back into the room. She carefully took Kristopher from my arms and placed him in his small and cozy looking basinet. We tiptoed out the room, Kai shutting the door behind her. We headed to the living room and I noticed that Toni was nowhere to be found. I assumed she probably headed back upstairs.

Kai and I took a seat in her living room; I sat on the couch as she curled up on her loveseat. I wasn't totally sure what I was going to say to her. I didn't really rehearse anything so I was definitely just going with what I was feeling.

"So how are you feeling?" I asked, not wanting to jump right into the serious stuff.

"I'm good, just a little sore and all, but the doctor says I will be 100% in a week or so."

"Oh good, good."

"Are we going to tiptoe around each other all night?" She asked as she pulled a blanket over her, "What's on your mind?"

"What makes you think something is on my mind?" I said, thinking there was a lot on my mind and I hated that she knew me so well.

"Because you always have something on your mind, Todd. Not to mention all of this going on."

"Yeah, this is a lot, a whole lot," I said and I suddenly lost my train of thought. I had so much I wanted to say, but didn't know how to go about it. I prepared speeches for a living to give in court, but for some reason, right then, I was not prepared at all for what I wanted to say. "I guess, I wanted to apologize to you."

"For what?" Kai asked as she kind of lifted her head a bit from the couch.

"For how I treated you when I found out that, well, that Riley was my daughter. And how I threw us away so fast." I took a deep breath; I needed a shot of courage in the form of Patron. Kai was silent. She didn't say a word, but just listened. I continued.

"I, um, I should have given us a second chance after what went down, I was just so devastated and never thought in a million years that you, well, that you would want to be with a woman, Alana of all women."

I cleared my throat and figured I just needed to throw everything into the ring. "Kai, I never thought I would feel the way I have felt in the last few days, seeing you and meeting our son for the very first time.

I'm overwhelmed with emotion and, well, and I'm just going to say this, because I am so nervous," I said with a chuckle in my voice, which helped relieve some of the pressure.

I pushed ahead and ignored the fear. "I want us to be a family, me and you and Kristopher. I know this is coming out of left field but believe me, I've never been more sure about anything in my life and I hope you can understand where I'm coming from." I stopped talking to take a few more breaths.

Kai sat up in her love seat and just looked at me for a few beats. "Why now?"

"Because now I realize what is important in life and that is you and what we had and you were right, I let Alana manipulate me and I know I should have listened to you, but I didn't but now I see her true self and, and I know that I made a big, big mistake and I… I want us to try again," I blustered.

"What about Riley, your daughter?"

"Well, that's another thing, crazy story…" I said and I felt myself getting nervous about telling Kai the truth. I stood, taking a moment to gather myself, since I knew this one was going to be hard to swallow for her. "I actually found out about a month ago that… well… that… Riley isn't really my child."

"What?" Kai said as she sat straight up, pulling the blanket off of her and putting it to the side. "Are you serious, Todd? I don't understand, I thought you took a paternity test?"

"I did, but the results came back to Alana as they did with you, and Alana forged the papers making it seem like I was the father even though I'm really not."

Kai kind of laughed and stood up, shaking her head. "You have got to be kidding me, are you serious?"

"Yes, very," I said, realizing how this must be coming off to her.

"So, let me get this straight. Riley is not your daughter because that manipulative bitch forged your paternity papers and in turn you leave me for her and your so-called child and now you expect me to just take you back because you felt a feeling this weekend? You have got to be out of your goddamn mind," Kai said coldly as she began walking out of the living room.

"Kai, please, I know this is crazy, but I want to be with you."

"Yeah, now, now that Riley isn't your daughter and you realized what a crazy ass bitch Alana is. I'm not a consolation prize, Todd."

"I know you're not. But you have to believe me, I made a mistake and I never should have left you for her, even if I thought we did have a child together."

"You are a piece of work, Todd, really." Kai ran her fingers through her mangled hair. "I think you'd better go."

"Kai, please."

"No, Todd, I can't digest this right now and I think it would be best if you just left now, please," Kai said as she walked over to the front door and opened it. "Please don't make me ask you again," Kai said in a softer tone.

I realized this was going to be an uphill battle, but I was prepared to fight for Kai and my son and what I knew was meant to be. I granted her wish and left, but I wasn't leaving New York until I won Kai, my son and her heart back.

Chapter 43
TODD

I lay in my bed in my hotel room replaying my conversation with Kai. I could understand where she was coming from and I knew from the jump that this wasn't going to be easy. Kai had a very valid point. I didn't try with her; I just threw in the towel for the sake of a daughter I thought was mine and a best friend I thought I could trust. But I had been wrong on both counts and now I would have to lie in the bed that I made for myself.

I wanted to call Kai, but since it had only been a few hours since I'd left her place, I thought it better to let her think about what I had just said. Hopefully tomorrow she would think differently. I knew it was a lot to digest for anyone.

I closed my eyes and Alana came to mind. She was probably going crazy since I had not called her in a few days. She would die if she knew I was in New York, but what she didn't know wouldn't hurt her. I would be home by the weekend hopefully, and I could let her know then that it was over between us for good and I would be moving out permanently.

My cell phone rang and I jumped towards it, hoping it was Kai calling. I looked down at the screen to see that it was Alana. I must have thought her up. I hesitated in answering it, but knew I couldn't avoid her forever.

"Hey, Alana," I said as I propped myself up on my pillow a bit.

"Wow, it's nice that you finally answered your phone, Todd," Alana said with an edge of attitude in her voice.

"Listen, Alana, I'm sorry I haven't called you back but I'm just busy taking care of some business."

"Oh, really and would that business be Kai-related?" Alana asked, continuing to dig into my situation.

"Alana, please, not now."

"If not now then when?" Alana wasn't going to stop.

"Listen, can I call you back? I'm in the middle of something right now."

"You are unbelievable," Alana said.

"I am unbelievable? You are the one who lied about Riley being my daughter, Alana," I said as I heard a silence on the other end.

"Todd, I'm sorry, I wanted to tell you, I was just so scared. I don't want to throw away what we have, what we built."

"What we built? Everything we have is built on lies."

"You just don't know how sorry I am. Baby, I want to start over, rebuild with you, and I know we can get through this, please. I can't sleep or eat. I'm not a bad person, you have to see that."

I lay my head back down, closing my eyes. "Alana, listen, in the next couple of days I will come by and we will talk, OK? Right now, I have to go."

"Why can't we talk today?"

"Because I can't, Alana."

"Why not," she pressured me, "What are you doing tonight that's so important you can't talk to me?"

Alana was really working my nerves. I knew what she was trying to do and I wasn't going to let her manipulate the conversation. Everything always had to be on her terms, but she had lost that privilege.

"I'm going to go now, and I will call you in a few days," I said and I hung up the phone, shaking my head. I wanted to call Kai, but knew that was not the best move, so I decided to, order up some room service and call it a night. Alana called back but I sent her to voicemail, turned my phone off and picked up the hotel phone to order a steak dinner. Tomorrow would be a new day and I wanted to be ready for whatever Kai was willing to throw at me, because I wasn't going down without a fight.

***

I tried Todd a few more times but realized he had turned his phone off. I was waiting for him to tell me that he was in New York visiting Kai, but I guess that was too much to expect. I threw my phone back into my purse, picked up my bags and got off the plane.

Surprising Todd by showing up in New York unannounced wouldn't sit well with him, but hey, he left me with no choice. I mean, you can't just leave and fly to another city without informing your significant other. I don't care if we aren't on the best terms - it's not acceptable in my book. If he didn't want to talk, I would just show up where he was at and then he would have no other choice. I knew the

logic was a bit off but hey, I really didn't have much
else to lose, did I?

I headed through the Delta terminal at JFK,
breezed past baggage claim and went outside. The
sound of the numerous honking cabs and shuttles and
cars made it impossible to hear myself think, so I
turned around and headed back inside the airport to
find a quieter place. I retrieved my phone once again
and dialed 411. I knew Kai lived in Brooklyn but I
didn't have her exact address. I was betting my last
dollar that Todd would be there when I arrived.

"411, may I help you?" the operator said.

"Yes, I'm looking for a phone number for Kai
Edwards in Brooklyn."

"Hold, please. Ma'am, I have a listing for a Kai
Edwards in Fort Green, would you like that?"

"Actually, can you just give me the address
instead?"

"Please hold for the address," the operator said. I
reached in my purse to grab a pen and something to
write on as an automated voice spoke Kai's address to
me. I quickly wrote it down and hung up the phone.

"Perfect," I said before heading back outside to
grab a cab to my hotel in Manhattan for some needed
R&R. I jumped in a cab and, after I told the driver
where I was going, I lay my head back and shut my
eyes. I finally got what I needed and it was time to
pay Kai and Todd a little visit.

Chapter 44
TODD

The next morning I got up, grabbed some
breakfast and coffee and headed back over to Kai's. It
was close to 10am and I figured Kai would be up by
now, seeing as she had a newborn and all.

I hopped on the train two blocks from my hotel
and took the twenty-minute ride to Brooklyn. After
getting off at the Adelphia exit, I stopped by a
neighborhood market and picked up a dozen flowers.
I thought it might be a nice touch or even a small
form of apology for the previous night. I continued

down the tree-lined streets of Fort Green until I turned onto the one where Kai lived.

I headed up the stairs of her brownstone and saw her friend Toni coming out of the doorway. There was something about this woman that I couldn't put my finger on, but I wasn't trying to figure that out since I had other things on my mind.

"Good morning," I said as Toni and I approached each other.

"Todd, I didn't expect you be back so soon."

Toni's comment threw me off. I wondered if Kai had shared our conversation with her from yesterday. "I'm actually coming by to say my goodbyes for now. I'm heading back to Chicago on the redeye tonight," I said, the lie falling out my mouth. I couldn't think of any other reason to tell her why I was back so soon without exposing my business.

"Oh, will you be coming back anytime soon?"

"I definitely plan on it, I just want to clear it with Kai, you know?" I said, trying to be as discreet as possible. Although, the way women talk, that might have been too little, too late.

"Is Kai up?" I asked.

"Oh, yeah, she's feeding Kristopher now. I left the door unlocked if you want to just go in. She shouldn't mind."

"Thanks, but I will knock," I said. "I don't want to scare her."

"Of course," Toni said with a smile as she passed me on the stairs. "I will be back... going to the store to pick up a few things." She hit the bottom of the stairway and headed down the street.

I continued up the stairs and knocked on Kai's front door but she didn't come. I knocked a bit harder thinking about the baby and hoping he had not fallen asleep, and how I didn't want to be the one to wake him. A few minutes passed when I finally looked up to see Kai holding Kristopher and opening the door for me. He was half asleep in her arms.

"Hey," I said trying to keep my voice down to a slight whisper.

"Todd, what are you doing here?"

"I, um, I came by to say goodbye, well, not goodbye like that, but goodbye for now. I am heading back to Chicago tonight, on the redeye," I said, thinking, there goes that lie again, but in that moment, I needed an excuse to get back into the house.

"Oh... um... OK. Well, did you want to come in for a minute?" Kai asked as she softly patted Kristopher on the back to burp him.

"Yeah, thanks," I said as Kai stepped aside to let me in. I was very nervous, and didn't really know what to say.

"I saw Toni on the way in, she said she was heading to the store. Did you need me to get anything for you?" I asked as we moved into her living room.

Kai just sat in her rocking chair and continued to attempt to burp our son. "No, we're good, really," Kai said, not really giving me too much eye contact. Maybe my visit back to her house was a mistake.

I watched as Kai fumbled with Kris a bit, trying to position him so that they were both comfortable. "Can I help you out with anything?" I asked, feeling kind of out of place, at the same time feeling like I should be doing something.

"Um, sure, I could use the break," Kai said as she stood and brought Kristopher over to me. "You remember what to do, right?"

"I may be new to this but I'm a quick learner." Kai put Kristopher in my arms and I instinctively put him over my shoulder and began to pat his back. "How am I doing?" I asked, looking back up at Kai.

"You're a pro." Kai said with a smile.

Finally Kristopher let out a nice sounding belch and within seconds I felt a warm sensation soaking through my shirt. "Please tell me he didn't—"

Kai got up and looked behind me. "Oh, yes, he did, my bad, I forgot to give you a burp cloth," she said as she laughed. "Welcome to Fatherhood. Think of it as your initiation of sorts."

"Yeah, thanks," I said as we both laughed.

"Hold on, let me grab a burp cloth to clean that off for you," Kai said as she disappeared to the back of the house.

I gently placed my son on my lap as his eyes were getting heavier and heavier. He was slowly drifting into a deep sleep. I was glad some of the tension was gone from yesterday's conversation. Maybe Kai had taken some time to think about what I'd said and processed this whole thing with us. I know I did. Then the doorbell rang, and I looked up to see where Kai had disappeared. "Hey, Kai, your doorbell, Kai?"

"Can you get it? It's probably Toni back from the corner store," Kai yelled from the back of the house.

"Sure," I said as I held Kris against my chest, stood and headed to the door, but when I opened it expecting to see Toni, I was floored to see Alana standing in the doorway. We just stared at each other for a moment.

"Oh how precious, father and son."

I was shocked to see Alana standing on Kai's porch, but not all that surprised. Alana is a woman who wasn't above stooping to the lowest of the lowest.

"Well, aren't you going to let me in?" Alana demanded as she stood there with a shitty ass look on her face.

"What the hell are you doing here?"

"Is that anyway to greet your girlfriend?" she replied.

I was so annoyed to see Alana, more than I could really say. "How did you find me?"

"Well, if you would call a sista back and not act so evasive I wouldn't have to go to these extremes to track your ass down."

"So now you're stalking me? Nice."

"Please, tracking people down is something I do in my sleep," Alana said with confidence in her voice. "Now, are you going to let me in or what?"

"Alana, I told you we would talk next week," I said firmly.

"Well, next week didn't work for me. I'm going to be tied up filming my movie. You would know that if you returned a phone call or two."

"Is that Toni?" Kai said as she walked up behind me. She stopped in her tracks when she saw Alana standing in her doorway.

"Hello, Kai," Alana said with a snarling smile on her face.

"What the hell are you doing here?" Kai demanded as she took Kristopher from my arms.

"Nice to see you too, Kai," Alana said.

"Sorry I can't say the same."

"Well, we all have our crosses to bear," Alana said as Kai let out a huge sigh.

"I have to put him down, you need to handle this," Kai said as she turned and walked away.

"Cute kid, you sure he's yours?" Alana asked.

"I know he's mine, I saw the original paternity test with my own eyes, unlike the one you gave me."

"Todd, I can explain about that," she said, "that's why I'm here."

"Alana, I can't talk to you now, I told you that on the phone."

"Why, because you're too busy playing house? Is that it?" Alana said as her voice began to tremble a bit. "Todd, if you leave me, I don't know what I'm going to do…"

I couldn't believe Alana. Showing up on Kai's doorstep like this and hitting me hard with the dramatics.

"I got to go, Alana," I said as I noticed Toni coming up the stairs behind her. Alana turned upon hearing the footsteps behind her. She moved aside when she saw Toni coming.

"And who might you be?" Alana asked with a sneer in her voice.

"I'm sorry? This is my property, so I think I should be asking you that question."

I interjected before Alana created yet another enemy, which was never hard for her to do. "Toni, this is Alana."

"Ah, so you're Toni," Alana said with a smirk.

"Excuse me?" Toni said.

"Yeah, what is that supposed to mean?" I asked.

"Oh, nothing. Well, Todd, I see you have your hands full here," Alana said as she eyed Toni up and down.

Toni shook her head and headed past us into the house.

"How well do you know that Toni woman?" Alana asked.

"Well enough, OK?"

"Hmm, well, if you ask me I think you need to do some probing around."

"Alana, what are you getting at now?" I said wearily.

"Just a word of advice, don't go throwing all your eggs in the Kai basket just yet, you might be surprised at what falls out."

"Alana," I said, "this conversation is over. I will talk to you when I get back to Chicago."

"Fine, but mark my words, you'll be coming back to me, and I won't even make you beg."

I had to laugh at Alana's confidence. "Yeah, don't hold your breath," I said as I closed the door on her and walked back into the living room. I sat back down on the couch as Kai came in.

"Care to explain what that was all about?" she asked.

"All I can say is that Alana has completely lost it. I'm sorry she just showed up on your doorstep like that."

"Well I can handle Alana," Kai said. "I mean I did give her her first broken nose."

"That you did." I sat back on the loveseat. "Alana is taking our breakup a bit hard."

"No, her ego is taking it hard." Kai chimed in.

"But believe me," I said, "I do not want to be with her anymore. I want to be with you." I said. I couldn't believe the words left my mouth so easily like that.

"Todd, please, I don't want to talk about us right now."

"Kai—"

"Todd, look," she interrupted, "I just don't want to deal with this, not today." She gave me a serious look and I knew I needed to back off.

"I guess I better go," I said.

"Yeah, I'm going to try and get some sleep before Kristopher wakes up."

"OK," I said.

"Have a safe flight back to Chicago," Kai said.

"Right… thanks," I said as I headed toward the door. I felt a strong wave of sadness flow over my body and I knew this couldn't be the end, but I didn't know what else to say or do. I wanted to stay until Kai finally gave in and took me back, but that wasn't going to happen, not right then anyway. I knew it would take some time.

"I guess I will call you tomorrow, just to check up on you guys."

"OK, sounds good," Kai said with a half smile followed by a yawn.

"Tell Toni I said bye and nice meeting her."

"I will."

I turned and headed out of the brownstone and down the stairs. As I walked and walked and walked, not realizing where I was going or where I would end up, I knew one thing for sure, I wasn't leaving New York without trying one last time to win back Kai's heart. I looked up from my reverie to see that I was standing in front of a café. I went in to grab a cup of coffee and sat at a small table near the back. I pulled out a pen and paper and began to pour my heart out to the woman I love.

***

I woke to the sound of Kristopher crying in his crib. I was tired as hell and could feel my body beginning to break down from sleep deprivation. I took a deep breath as I swung my feet off the bed, hitting the cold wood floor. I located my pink slippers before attempting to walk across the room to pick up my son.

It was 5 in the morning, which meant it was feeding time. I headed to the kitchen and gently placed Kris in his bouncy chair before grabbing a cold bottle of breast milk from the fridge. I placed it in the

bottle warmer and leaned back against the counter
when I noticed an envelope sitting on my kitchen
table with my name on it. I walked over and picked it
up and examined it closely. It was a letter from Todd.
I wondered how it got here, and could only conclude
that Todd had brought it back after he left, while I was
taking a nap, slipping it under my door for Toni to
grab. I placed the letter under my arm, grabbed the
warm bottle of milk and sat down next to Kristopher
to feed him his breakfast.

I read the words that Todd had felt were so
important for me to see.

Dear Kai,

Please forgive me for leaving without saying
goodbye but the longer I spend with you and Kris the
harder it is for me to leave New York. I told myself
that I wasn't going to return to Chicago without a
commitment from you, but I quickly came to the
realization that a decision like that will take time. Kai,
I am aware that I dumped a lot on you the other day
and I know it was a lot to digest, but believe me when
I say this... I meant every word of it. We have
definitely been through a lot in the last few years,
both of us making mistakes along the way, but the one
thing that I regret in the midst of our wrongdoing is
that we didn't try to work it out... I didn't try to work

it out, and that is one thing I truly regret. I made a lot of hasty decisions and foolish assumptions and now I am reaping the consequences. You and Kristopher are my future and I know this from the bottom of my heart and I hope one day you will feel the same way.

I'm a big believer that time heals all wounds and our time is coming, you just need time to heal and I respect that and I am willing to step back and let that happen. Now please do not misconstrue this, I'm not saying all this because of Riley not truly being my daughter but for the pure fact that I love you! Always have, always will, Kai. I made a mistake but I want to make it right and be a family. I know this could work and I know we would be so happy together.

I love you more than you know, Todd

I slowly put the letter down and felt a few tears trying to escape. A sense of relief flowed over my body. I knew I needed to hear those words from Todd. I did love him, but I hated what had happened to us in our past. I'd never meant to hurt him with my affair with Alana and sure didn't expect things to end the way that they did. I really did want a family and knew there was no better man to have one with than the man who had help create the perfect bundle I was cradling in my arms. Todd was right, we had both made mistakes, and now we must find a way to forgive each other if that was truly for the best. I looked down at my sleeping son as I laid him back down in his crib before sliding back into bed. I felt myself drifting off to sleep, but not before smiling at the thought that Todd could be mine again, and all I had to do was say the word.

Chapter 45
TODD

I was tying up some loose ends in the office after being away for a few days. I had only been back home for a day and knew I needed to finalize things with Alana. But when I called to set something up, her voicemail said she would be in New York for the next two weeks shooting her newest film. That was a bit of relief, as I could really pull everything together and even move some things out the condo before she returned.

I heard a faint knock at my door. I looked up to see Jessica standing in my doorway. At first I didn't totally recognize her since when I met her I was a bit intoxicated. She looked pretty much the same as I could remember, although seeing her in the day felt kind of weird, not to mention I was curious to know what had brought her there to see me.

"I'm sorry to just drop in on you like this but I really needed to talk to you."

I stopped what I was doing and stood. "Um, no problem, come in," I said as I walked around my desk to the middle of my office, meeting her half way.

"I know this is a bit weird and maybe somewhat awkward but I really needed to get something off my chest," Jessica said as I motioned for her to take a seat on my black leather couch. She sat down and I joined her by sitting in the chair just to her right. She seemed very uncomfortable, which in turn made me feel uncomfortable. I could only imagine she wanted to talk about Alana and that could never be good.

"So, what's on your mind?" I asked in an upbeat tone, trying to keep the mood lighter than it really was.

Jessica sat up and crossed her legs, then looked directly at me. " I think you need to know something. The night we met and we had our threesome with you and Alana, well, that wasn't the first time I had been intimate with your girlfriend. We'd been seeing each other for a while by then."

I sat back upon hearing this. "And what constitutes a while?"

"About three months."

I was quiet. I didn't have anything to say for I was still processing the "three months" part. But then the obvious question came up for me. "Why are you telling me this?"

Jessica continued. "Because I think you need to know what type of woman you are dealing with."

"Jessica, despite you being here and telling me all this, I know the kind of woman I am dealing with. But I thank you for coming in," I said and stood, thinking I could really give a damn and that hearing all this didn't surprise me one bit."There's more," Jessica said staring at me. She quickly looked away when our eyes connected.

I sat back down. "I'm listening."

"I'm in love with her," Jessica said, looking back up at me.

"Excuse me?

"I know it sounds crazy but there's something about her that I can't let go of."

I had to laugh out loud after hearing those words come out of Jessica's mouth. "Yeah, it's called manipulation," I said. "Wow, the wrath of Alana strikes again. So you're not here to warn me about

Alana, but to let me know you want to be with her. Is that correct?"

"I know it sounds crazy but…"

"It's OK, you can have her. I was done with her before you even opened your mouth," I said standing up again. As far as I was concerned this conversation was done. "Jessica, thank you for coming in, but honestly, I have nothing left to say to you two but good luck."

"Are you going to tell Alana I was here?"

I thought about her question, and then figured what was the point, I didn't care anymore. "No, I'm not. For what it's worth, I hope you two are happy together."

Jessica stood, nodded gratefully towards me and left my office. I sat back down behind my desk as I leaned way back on my reclining chair and placed both of my hands behind my head and thought, How on earth does Alana do it? This poor woman was in love with her and I know Alana didn't give a rat's ass about her.

Chapter 46
KAI

After everything that went down with Alana and Todd I knew I needed to pay my therapist a visit. I got Toni to watch Kristopher for a few hours so I could go see Dr. Albright. I had a lot on my mind since Todd had poured his heart out to me in his heartfelt letter but I was still uncertain about getting back together with him. Although I'm sure Todd's intentions were good, I needed a second opinion to put my mind at ease, and I knew of no better opinion than my therapist's.

"So how is the baby?" Dr. Albright asked the moment I walked into her office.

"He's good, just cries a lot."

"Well, that's what babies do."

"Yes, indeed," I said as I smiled and sat down on her leather chaise, quickly assuming my favorite position, which was flat on my back.

"I didn't expect to see you so soon after the baby," Dr. Albright said. "How is everything going in your life?"

"Kind of complicated," I said slowly.

"OK, well 'complicated' isn't too descriptive, but I'm sure we can get to the bottom of it," Dr. Albright said as she pulled out her yellow pad and wrote a few words across the top.

I took a deep breath as I stared at Dr. Albright's ceiling, then looked at the wall, wondering if she had painted since I had been there last. Her walls were a natural camel color with white trim around the crown molding that lined the top. I could've sworn that the last time I was in there her walls were mauve.

"Todd told me that he wants me back. I mean, he wants to start over, have a family with me."

"All right. What do you want?"

"Well, I do want a family, especially now that I have a son, but—"

Dr. Albright was quiet, so I turned to look at her, assuming she would say something but instead she just smiled at me saying, "Go on."

"I just don't want to make a mistake."

"By taking him back?" Dr. Albright asked.

"Yes."

"Do you truly love this man?" she asked.

My first initial reaction was to say, Yes, I do, very much, but then my ego stepped in, interjecting feelings from the past, screaming, I do but how could he have picked Alana over me? Ever?

"Yes, I do," I said, sitting up on my elbows, "but what I guess I can't get over is how he just threw me away for Alana. That hurt me so much."

"I'm sure it did, Kai, but from what you've told me, Todd thought he was doing the right thing and it was coming after you had hurt by with your affair with Alana. Humans have a funny way of expressing hurt and anger and I'm sure him rejecting you was his way of dealing with that."

I lay back down on my back to absorb what Dr. Albright had just said.

"Kai, don't make your decision from a place of hurt and deceit, make it from a place of truth and love. If you truly love Todd then your answer is there. The past is just that, the past, and there is nothing you or I can do to change what has happened. What counts..." she said, "is how we live our lives from here on out."

I turned to look at Dr. Albright as she took her glasses off and gave me a smile. "I think you know what you want do, I just think that you're scared, and that's perfectly fine. But don't deny Todd his second chance to make it right, because I would hate for you to wake up tomorrow, or next month or even next year, wishing you had given him the chance to help you build your family."

I lay very still on Dr. Albright's chaise. I felt so comfortable just being there. I let what she said absorb into my being as I analyzed her walls again, coming to the conclusion that she did change the paint color and that I definitely liked it better than the old. The past is the past and maybe a new paint job would do me just fine.

I headed out of the doctor's office with a clear vision of my future and, for the first time in ages, it made me smile. I grabbed my phone and texted Todd, telling him that I got his letter and I agreed that we should try again. Todd got back to me within minutes with a message that he was so happy to hear that, and how he could be back in New York the next week to talk about it in more detail. I sent him back a smiley face and the letter 'K' before putting my phone back into my purse and heading home to my son and soon-to-be-new life.

Chapter 47
ALANA

My unexpected visit to Kai's house in New York
was my way of saying; I am not done, not even close.
Todd may have thought that he wanted to be with Kai,
but the truth was, Kai was boring and so not the
woman for him and he knew that, he was just
confused. It was up to me to set him straight. I
decided to head back to Chicago after Emanuel texted
me to say that my movie shoot had been pushed
ahead a month, something about the starting day
conflicting with the lead actor's schedule. What about

my damn schedule? I thought, but I figured I couldn't complain, as I wasn't the star—yet.

My flight landed at 3:30 in the afternoon and I was supposed to meet Emanuel for dinner at six. My agent and I had become close friends despite our sometimes stormy working relationship and I truly appreciated his friendship.

Emanuel entered the restaurant like a breath of fresh air, sporting a pair of tight jeans and a pink button-up shirt. My guess was that he had a date soon after our dinner was over. It must pay to be gay because he got more booty than I could ever imagine.

"Well, look at you? Pretty in pink." I said as Emanuel pranced in, placed a kiss on my cheek and sat down across from me at the table. He seemed very relaxed and content. I guess that's what multiple orgasms would do for you.

"Oh, thank you, child, just trying to keep my appearance up so I can keep turning the boys' heads."

"When are you going to settle down with one guy?" I asked as I grabbed the menu to see what I could order.

"Child, please, there is too much candy I haven't tasted yet in this candy store," Emanuel said, drawing an imaginary circle with a round motion snap, a recognizable gay gesture in any country.

I forgot that Emanuel had only been in Chicago for a little over a year. When his father opened their agency here in the city, he sent Emanuel to Chicago to run it. And a cardinal rule for the gay men I've met is that you do not want to settle down until you have perused the whole store, so to speak.

"Well, speaking of settling down, I think I found your next husband," Emanuel said with a smile.

I looked up from my menu with confusion on my face. "Husband? I don't want to meet anyone new," I said. "Todd and I are going to work through this, he's just taking a little bit longer to come around."

"Child, please, are you listening to yourself? You told me yourself he found the paternity test results, not to mention your little performance of following him to Kai's house in New York. Honey, I may be slow at times but that man is moving on."

I felt a bit of irritation at Emanuel's comments rising from my inner being. "No, Todd just needs sometime to pull it together, he will come to his senses and realize that he belongs with me."

Emanuel sat back and crossed his arms across his chest. "What is your obsession with this man, honey?"

"Please, there is no obsession, we belong together. Clearly you will never understand what we have, OK?"

"Clearly you are a bit delusional."

"Call it what you want," I said, "but you will see when we are back together once and for all."

"Fine," Emanuel said, "but I just think you should throw your net overboard and see what else is out there. It won't kill you."

"Listen, I know you're trying to help, but this is not something I need for you to resolve for me. Todd will come around, he always does," I said with a snarl in my voice, making sure he got the damn hint. I felt my body temperature rise a bit more and I reached for my wine glass and finished off the rest of the glass in one swallow.

"OK," Emanuel said, rolling his eyes as he unfolded his arms.

"And in the meantime," I added, "I will entice him bit."

"And how do you plan on doing that, exactly?"

I dug into my purse and pulled out two plane tickets. "Todd has always wanted to go to Greece, so I took the liberty of booking us a 10-day trip there."

"Wow, well, that's something," Emanuel said in a dull tone.

"You don't think this is a great idea?"

"I don't think buying him a trip will win him back. Listen sweetheart…" he went on, "I know you think you have this all figured out, but this is not the way to get him back. Alana, honey, you lied, deceived and manipulated him. I hate to sound harsh but you're going to have to come up with something better than a round-trip ticket to Greece."

"You know what," I said feeling the anger rise up. "Clearly you don't understand my situation. You're definitely not on my side and this dinner is over! If you can't be supportive of me and Todd trying to work it out then obviously I mistook you for a true friend and definitely made a mistake making you my agent. You're fucking fired," I said getting up to leave.

"Alana, wait, just sit back down," he pleaded.

"Go to hell, Emanuel!" I headed out the restaurant and heard Emanuel calling out my name. I looked down at the tickets to Greece and I felt for a moment that maybe there was something true about what Emanuel had said to me. Maybe he was right... but then again, maybe he wasn't. My mind was racing a mile a minute trying to decipher what was right and what was wrong.

I jumped in my car and sat there for a minute, slowly realizing in my heart of hearts that I was going to lose Todd. I could feel him slipping from my grip and that enraged me to no end. But what was really sending me over the top was where he was slipping to, and that was to Kai.

Little Miss Perfect always gets what she wants, I thought. Believe you me, she is not getting this, not if I can fucking help it. I threw the tickets on the passenger seat. I needed to do something, something drastic that would make Todd mine forever.

Chapter 48
KAI

The day Kristopher turned three weeks old I was ready to take him out the house - not to mention I was getting a bit of cabin fever and needed to feel more than my mahogany floors under my feet. Toni was home from her morning class so I asked if she wanted to join us, and she joyfully agreed. The three of us headed to the park about two blocks away where there was a playground, a wishing fountain and plenty of fresh grass to spread a blanket and bask in the beautiful day that was upon us. In the previous couple of weeks since Toni had been there for me, I realized that I really didn't know a whole lot about her, but it felt like she knew my whole life inside and out. When it came to her, though, I felt like I didn't know her, at least not the inner her. Maybe our time today would be a good time to really dig deep into what this woman was all about.

"How was your class?" I asked.

"It was good, yeah, I have some very intelligent students this semester, so I'm happy about that."

"That's good," I said as I covered Kris up a bit with his blanket. "Toni, I don't think I've ever told you how appreciative I am for all your help."

"Oh, please, it's my pleasure. I live a simple life, not too much excitement going on over here."

I smiled at Toni's view on her life, although I was sure her life was nowhere near as simple as she made it out to be. Sometimes people downplay aspects of their lives so they won't have to talk about things, and that's the feeling I got from Toni.

"You know," I said, "ever since I met you, I've been dumping all my issues on you and now I realize that I don't really know that much about you, and I feel bad."

"Like I said, my life is nothing to talk about, really. I enjoy listening to you, believe me," Toni said with a smile.

"But I don't know anything about you, like, what was your childhood like? Are you an only child or do you have siblings? I don't even know where you went to law school, if teaching was a passion of yours or if you just found yourself in it one day."

Toni smiled and adjusted herself on the blanket. She started to look a little uncomfortable. "I've never been big on talking about my life."

"Why not?" I asked.

"It's just, um, it's just something I never really did. Why would I want to burden you with my life?" Toni asked as she smiled and turned her attention toward Kristopher. "I think he's hungry. You brought bottles of course, right?"

I put my hand on top of Toni's, stopping her from grabbing the bottles—and changing the subject.

"Because we're friends, that's why, and friends share their lives with each other. But I don't want to make you feel uncomfortable. I was just trying to get to know my friend." I pulled out a burp cloth and a bottle and started to feed Kristopher. I figured I shouldn't press the issue, and just be happy that Toni was in my life.

"I was married for 10 years, but I learned that in life some things just don't work out," Toni said, catching me off guard.

I looked over at her. "What happened?

"Well, I fell in love with a woman who broke my heart," Toni said as she looked up and smiled at me.

"A woman?" I repeated.

"Yes, I'm a lesbian."

"Why didn't ever tell me that?"

"I didn't want to make you feel uncomfortable,"

I had to laugh. "Me uncomfortable? Are you kidding? As much as I have revealed to you, why would you think that telling me you're a lesbian would make me feel uncomfortable?"

"Because I'm a lesbian who is in love with you."

My stomach did a flip upon hearing these words. That had to be the very last thing in the world that I expected to come out of her mouth. OK, now I was definitely uncomfortable.

"You're in love with me?" I repeated, just making sure I'd heard Toni correctly.

"See, you're uncomfortable," she said.

"No, no, I'm, I'm not, not really."

"Yes," Toni said, "you are, but that's OK. The last thing I wanted to do was make you uncomfortable." She stood as if to leave.

"Where are you going?" I asked.

"I'd better go."

"No," I said, "don't, please. Believe me when I say this, I'm not uncomfortable."

"Yeah, but now I feel uncomfortable," Toni said with her familiar soft smile. "We'll talk later." She turned and walked away.

I sat there trying to process what had just happened, and hated that I had gone there with her. I hoped I hadn't lost a good friend.

Chapter 49
TODD

I was finalizing my trip back to New York to see
Kai and Kris, and had a feeling of pure excitement as
I printed out my airline confirmation. I knew what I
was doing was right thing to do and I couldn't wait to
sit down and talk all of it over with Kai. I wondered if
she would be willing to move back to Chicago or
maybe I could open up a satellite practice in New
York. I had a lot of ideas swirling around in my head.
I felt like a giddy kid thinking about all that lay ahead
of us as a family.

My mind then shifted to Alana who had been calling me non-stop since she'd been back in town, and I had yet to return one of her phone calls. I was surprised she hadn't simply popped up at my office, but then again she may have, since I had been in court most of my time back. I really needed to end it with her once and for all.

Separating myself from Riley would be the hardest part, but it had to be done. I couldn't keep any ties with Alana; it wouldn't work if I wanted to build something real with Kai. I picked up my phone to call Alana when Maceo entered my office. I had not seen him in a few weeks so I postponed my call to Alana to speak to him.

"Hey, welcome back," Maceo said as he walked in and sat down in front of me.

"Thanks," I said, "and it's good to see you, too, Maceo."

"So, what's the word? How was New York?"

"New York was good," I said, "Alana showed up at Kai's house."

"Are you serious, yo? How in the hell did she find you?"

"I have no damn idea, the whole situation was bananas," I said, shaking my head just thinking about it all again.

"Damn," Maceo said, "talk about a bitch who will not go down for the count."

"Tell me about it."

"What did you do?" he asked.

"I told her to leave and that we'd talk when I got back to Chicago. Of course, typical Alana, trying to start a scene."

"Damn," said Maceo. "You know, she swung by here a few times when you were gone, but I didn't tell her ass anything."

"Yeah, I figured. Thanks for covering, but it is time for me to end this once and for all with her. What Alana did was unforgivable." I said. "I don't even want to look at her ass anymore. I am so done it is not funny, and the sooner I get it over with, the sooner I can move forward with my life with Kai and my son."

"So you two are going to work it out?"

"That's the plan. I mean, we have a lot of things to work through, but I feel good about this." I said.

"Cool, cool, well, of course I wish you all the luck in the world. When are you heading back?"

"Tomorrow night," I replied, "so I need to talk to you about the workload."

"Listen," he said firmly, "I will cover it, and if I can't, I'll pull in a friend of mine who just got laid off from his firm. Go handle your biz."

"Thanks, man," I said as Maceo stood.

"I better get back to work," he said, "but hit me if you need me."

"Will do."

Maceo headed out my office and I was reaching for my phone to call Alana when it started ringing, showing an unknown number. I figured it was a client or the courthouse.

"This is Todd Daniels."

"Hello, Mr. Daniels, this is Ernestine Clark calling from Northwestern Memorial Hospital."

"OK?" I said wondering what this could be about.

"An Alana Brooks asked us to call you."

"Alana?"

"Yes, Mr. Daniels, she has been seriously injured you may want to get down here as soon as possible."

"What happened?" I said, feeling a sense of panic coming over me.

"The doctor can fill you in when you arrive."

"I'm on my way," I said as I hung up the phone. With one movement I grabbed my coat and was out the door. In that moment nothing seemed more important than Alana's safety. I was hoping she was OK.

Chapter 50
KAI

I was missing Toni. It had been few days since
she'd told me she was in love with me and I hadn't
stopped thinking about it since. Her feelings for me
definitely made me take a step back and think about
my intentions and my feelings for her. I thought about
my relationship with Alana and always looked at it as
a one-time thing, and I never thought I could have
feelings for another woman again. But Toni was so
different than Alana, she was loving and caring and
kind and giving. She had all the attributes Alana never

could possess, all the attributes that made returning her love seem easy.

I took a deep breath and stretched my body as I relaxed on my living room couch. Kristopher had finally settled down for his nap and was sleeping in his crib. I didn't realize how exhausting being a mom could be. Your time is no longer your own and that was something I was getting used to fast.

I closed my eyes and tried to get some well-needed sleep before being summoned for a feeding or a changing, but I kept thinking about Toni. It was killing me and I had to address it. I grabbed my phone, pulling up her number and shot her a text: Hey Toni, you awake?

I sat my phone down and stared at it, waiting for her instant response. Seconds felt like minutes and finally I heard that familiar beep that alerted me that I had a message. I grabbed my phone and read Toni's text message: Yes, I am. How are you doing?

I texted her back: Tired but good, can you come down… to talk?

She answered in seconds: Sure, be there in ten.

I jumped up and ran to the bathroom to evaluate my appearance. I had to stop myself and laugh because Toni has seen me at my worst, so why was I concerned as to how I looked now? Oh, my God! I was in love with this woman and hadn't realized it until she'd revealed it to me.

I felt my head starting to spin, thinking, but I'm in love with Todd—or am I? I splashed my face with cold water before grabbing my mouthwash from my cabinet and gargling. I didn't know what to expect when I saw Toni, all I knew was that we needed to talk. I was in the middle of changing my top when Toni rang the doorbell. I took one last glance in the mirror before heading to the front door to let her in.

"Hey," I said as I slowly opened the door.

"Hey, yourself," Toni shot back accompanied her greeting with a warm smile.

Toni headed in and I closed the door behind her. Her visit felt like it was the first time all over again. . Then again, after I thought about it, I guess I was meeting her for the first time under these new circumstances.

"Is the little one sleeping?" Toni asked as she sat down on my couch and crossed her legs. She looked pretty comfortable, which was good in a way. I walked over to move my cover and pillow out of her way.

"Yes, finally, he's been kind of cranky all day, so hopefully he will sleep through the night," I said as I folded up my blanket, tossing it into my chocolate leather ottoman along with my pillow. "Can I get you a drink or something to eat?"

Toni kind of chuckled. "This is pretty awkward, huh?"

"Oh, God, yes!" I said as I plopped down on the couch. Her comment had managed to break through some very thick ice.

"I didn't tell you what I told you to make it awkward between the two of us, really. I could have kept this a secret, but you're right... I don't share a lot of my life with people and that is something I have to start to change," she said.

"I guess I didn't help much with pushing the issue, huh?" I said.

"Pretty much, but it's all good, mama."

"So now what?" I asked.

"Now we move past this. Believe me, this is not a first for me and probably won't be the last. I fall for people kind of fast, especially if they are as amazing as you," Toni said with a smile. I didn't know what to say to that.

Toni stood up. "I'd better go before it gets uncomfortable again.

I stood, too. "Actually, I don't want you to go," I said as I walked closer to her.

"I mean, if you have to you have to, it's just..."

"What Kai?"

I took a deep breath; my stomach felt weird, fluttery. "It's just..." And before I knew it I leaned in and kissed her on the lips. Toni just stood there, probably just as confused as I was.

"OK, now I'm confused," Toni said with a nervous laugh.

"Yeah, me too," I said, "but one thing I'm clear about is that I don't want to lose you."

"You'll never lose me," she said. "I told you, I'm here for you, always."

Hearing Toni say that made me want her even more and I reached out, taking her hand, and we began to kiss again, this time more passionately. Toni and I fell back down on the couch and she caressed my face as we kissed. She was a great kisser and it felt as if she were in this 100%. My mind was racing, but her touch felt good as she continued to caress my entire body.

Toni stopped and looked at me. "Are you OK with this, Kai?"

"I am," I said, and we continued to kiss and caress each other's bodies. We ended up making love that night and I never thought about Todd, not once.

***

I jumped up startled to the sound of Kristopher crying. It was 2am and just like clockwork my son was ready for his feeding. I rolled over to see Toni fast asleep next to me and I took a deep breath before retrieving my son.

As I grabbed Kris from his crib, I noticed that I had a text message from Todd:

Hey beautiful, just thinking about you, can't wait to see you and Kristopher and hopefully spend the rest of our lives together.

Todd's text instantly put everything in perspective and made me "second think" what I had just done with Toni. I quickly fed and burped Kris, then changed and cuddled with him for a while before putting him back down to sleep. It was now 3:30am and Toni was still fast asleep when I quietly slid back into my bed. I turned to look at her as my movement jarred the bed and she slowly opened her eyes.

"Hey, what time is it?" Toni asked as she smiled at me.

"It's only 3:30 am, go back to sleep," I said, starting to feel the guilt engulf my being.

Toni pushed herself up, leaning back on my headboard.

We were both quiet. Toni finally broke the silence, asking, "So how do you feel about what happened last night?"

"A little confused, but I don't regret it, really, it's just…"

"Todd. I know. Listen, Kai, the last thing I want to do is get between you and Todd, especially since you two have a child together. Believe me, I didn't come down here last night to sleep with you."

"I know, and I didn't assume that. I'm just a little confused and maybe my confusion led me to do what I did."

I slowly sat up and crossed my arms over my chest. "I love Todd, but I also don't want to lose you, either."

"Hey, I told you from the jump, I'm not going anywhere, whatever we decide to do. But I think you need time to really think about what you really want out of life because each decision you make will impact you in a very different way."

"Yeah, I know," I said, wondering how in the hell I had managed to get myself in this situation again.

"I think you're an amazing woman and whatever decision you decide to make I'm sure it will be the right one for you," Toni said as he slid out of my bed and put on her clothes.

"You're leaving?"

"Yeah, I'm going to get an early start and hit the gym. Besides, you need some time to think," Toni said as she leaned over and kissed me gently on the lips. "Call me if you need me."

"OK."

I slid back down into my covers and listened as Toni headed down the hallway and out the front door. I knew what I did was taking a chance, especially since Todd was on his way to New York to talk about our future. I thought about how devastated he would be if I told him I wanted to be with Toni and not with him, a familiar feeling for him that he might never recover from. I closed my eyes tightly, hoping the answer would just hit me like a brick but the harder I tried to make it come, the farther away it felt. The only thing that came to me was a hefty serving of guilt, and the thought, Oh God, what have I done now?

Chapter 51
TODD

I didn't know what to expect when I got to the hospital. The person who'd called me hadn't been clear on what exactly had happened to Alana. I pulled into the visitors' garage, headed into the north tower taking the elevator to the 8th floor. I walked up to the nurses' station to find out where Alana was.

A petite young woman directed me down the hall to room 842. She explained that Alana was slightly incoherent and would need to rest soon. I slowly walked into Alana's room as I heard the beeps of the machines that were monitoring her vitals. Alana lay on the sterile, white bed, very still, with her face turned toward the window. I couldn't tell at that angle if she were asleep or awake.

"Alana?" I said softly as I carefully approached her bedside. She turned her head toward the sound of my voice and slowly opened her eyes.

"Hey, you. Thanks for coming."

Alana had thick white gauze across her head as well as a broken arm, from what I could see.

"Alana, what happened?" I asked, as I got a bit closer, evaluating her injuries.

Alana eyes immediately began to tear up. "I got robbed, baby, right outside our condo. He hit me in the head, took my purse. I tried to get up, to see his face, but I guess I lost my balance and fell down the stairs." Alana let out a weak cough. "The next thing I knew I woke up here, in the hospital and the only person I could think of was you."

"Oh, my God, I'm so sorry," I said as I rubbed her hair with my hand.

"I needed you, baby, this wouldn't have happened if you'd been with me."

"Where was Riley?" I asked.

"She's with another parent from school. I hadn't picked her up yet so they called the school to let them know what had happened."

I breathed a sigh of relief hearing the news that Riley was OK. "I am so sorry this happened to you. Is there anything I can do?" I asked, feeling terrible seeing Alana in that condition.

Alana reached out her good hand, sliding it into mine. "I need you to stay with me for a while, just until I can get back on my feet," Alana said, as she squeezed my hand tightly.

"I… um… I'm actually headed out of town tomorrow night," I said, feeling a little bad all of a sudden.

"Baby," she pleaded, "I need you so much right now. I need help with Riley. I can't do this alone."

I took a deep breath, thinking, this is not good. Here I am supposed to leave tomorrow to be with Kai, and Alana is begging me to stay. I didn't know what to do, what to think, but Alana was definitely in need and her bruises where real.

"I know we've been through a lot but please don't leave me now. Please…" Alana said, begging me as the tears flowed down her face.

"I will be right back, I need to make a few calls," I said and headed out into the hallway, trying to think of what I could tell Kai. Maybe that this was something that I needed to keep to myself. Kai wouldn't understand and everything I had been building with her in the last few weeks would be ruined. I leaned against the wall as I contemplated what the hell to do. I felt so damn torn and this could not have happened at a worse time. I thought about Kai and her response. Yep, I concluded, this is something I definitely have to keep under my hat.

***

I watched as Todd walked out of my hospital room. I turned my head back toward the window and felt a momentary sense of relief. I knew his out-of-town business had everything to do with Kai and that was something I needed to put a stop to. Once Todd committed to staying and taking care of me, it would only be a matter of time before he was mine again. We belonged together and he knew that, and Kai could never give him what I could. I took a deep breath and smiled, thinking how I had Todd wrapped around my finger. He was out there right at that moment, trying to decide what to do, thinking of ways to make it work, figuring out how to take care of me and what to tell Kai—if anything. Todd just needed a little nudge sometimes and I was the woman who could give him just that.

Chapter 52
KAI

I had mixed feelings after hearing that Todd had to stay in Chicago for a few more days. As he had put it, "Something suddenly came up." That "something suddenly" had Alana written all over it. I'd never put anything past her, not at all. Alana was and would always be a conniving bitch and because of that, I despised the day she ever walked into my or Todd's life. The one thing Todd and I would have to make clear once we got together was that he would need to cut all ties with Alana if he wanted to be with me.

Contact with her would be a huge deal-breaker for me, that is, if I decided to move forward with Todd instead of being with Toni.

I picked up my phone to call Simone. I needed to fill her in on everything that was happening. I was tired but I needed to talk to my best friend.

"Hey there, I was just thinking about you," Simone said as she picked up her phone. "What's going on with you?"

"Do you have a few minutes?" I asked.

"Of course. How are you and Todd doing?"

"Well, that's what I wanted to talk to you about. A few things have happened since I talked to you."

"What's going on?" she asked.

"Well, remember my landlord, Toni?"

"Of course, the lesbian lady," Simone said without missing a beat.

"What do you mean, 'the lesbian lady'? You knew she was a lesbian?"

"Oh, I could tell she was gay the moment I met her," she replied.

"What?" I exclaimed. "Are you serious? I never got that vibe from her."

"Of course you didn't," Simone said. "Don't tell me she hit on you."

"Damn, do you have a camera set up in my place?"

"Kai, it didn't take a rocket scientist to see that she wanted you. So how hard did she hit you up?" Simone asked with a chuckle.

"Pretty hard. She told me she was in love with me."

"Wow, she went there?" Simone said. "Screw the I'm-kind-of-attracted-to-you line and go in for the kill. So what did you say?"

"I slept with her."

"That much, huh? Well, at least you got the whole 'I wonder how it would be to sleep with you?' thing out the way real fast. So now what?"

"Oh, God, I don't know, I can't believe I am back in this place again. I feel like I haven't progressed one bit. I need time to process this, her, us, everything."

"Isn't Todd on his way back to New York for you guys to work things out?"

"Yeah, that was the plan."

"Don't tell me you called him and told him not to come," Simone said.

"No, he actually beat me to the punch."

"What do you mean?" she asked.

"I get a call from him today saying something suddenly came up and he won't be able to make it for a few days. And I'm thinking that 'something' has to do with Alana."

"Oh, but of course," Simone said, quickly agreeing with me.

"Maybe this is a sign?"

"A sign for what, Kai?"

"That maybe I shouldn't be with Todd but with Toni." Simone was quiet, which kind of made me nervous. "Are you there?" I asked making sure we didn't get disconnected.

"I'm here," Simone finally chimed in.

"So what do you think?" I asked.

"I think you are getting ahead of yourself. Do you really want to go down that path again with a woman, seriously?"

I had to stop and really analyze her question, as I wasn't sure what I wanted right then. "I don't know."

"Well, my advice? Don't make any rash decisions, think about what you would be doing and think about your future—and, of course, your son."

What Simone was saying was so true. I had to think about what kind of life I wanted to lead, and figure out if the thing with Toni was just an infatuation. Am I just mixing up my feelings? I wondered to myself.

"Remember," Simone continued, "you and Todd had something special before Alana walked her ass up into the middle of your lives and now I don't want you to blow it for the second time because maybe you are kind of lonely, and a lot horny, living out there all alone."

"Tell me how you really feel," I said and we shared a laugh.

"Hey, if your best friend can't be honest with you who can, right?"

"Yeah, that's so true," I said. "I better go and take a nap before Kristopher wakes up."

"OK darling, call me later."

"I will," I said as I hung up the phone. I was only going to rest for a few minutes, but before I knew it, I was woken up by my doorbell. At first I thought it was a dream, but quickly realized that it was real. I stumbled out of bed, threw on my robe and headed out my bedroom and for the front door. I couldn't believe my eyes when I opened the door to see Patrick standing there. It was a bittersweet moment as we stood there just staring at each other for a second. Then we gently embraced and before we ended our embrace Patrick was crying. "I am so sorry Kai, my intentions where not to hurt you."

"I know, I know. And I hope you can understand why I couldn't see you for a while, but I'm glad you are here now because I really did miss you."

"I missed the hell out of you," Patrick said wiping away his tears.

"Come in please," I said stepping back and letting him come in.

"No... I um... I can't actually. I'm actually late for class but was in your neighborhood and..."

"Just wanted to stop by," I said finishing Patrick's sentence, laughing because that was typical Patrick.

We stared at each other for a minute.

"So, I will call you?" Patrick asked with hesitancy.

"Yes, please and you have to come back to meet my son"

"Oh, it would be my pleasure to meet your son. How is the father?"

"We'll talk," I said with a smile.

Patrick returned my smile, "Hmm sounds interesting.

"To say the least..." I said wondering if I should share my encounter with Toni with Patrick. I quickly vetoed that idea since she was his professor and Toni would probably kill me.

"Well have a good class and I look forward to your call and visit."

"Ditto," Patrick said as he gave me a friendly wink, turned and headed down the steps of my brownstone. As I watched Patrick head down the street I thought about how funny life could be, and wondered why God brought Patrick back into my life. Well, I guess I will just have to wait and find out.

Chapter 53
TODD

I didn't know what it was but something felt weird about Alana's situation. I didn't know if I was just so used to her being so damn manipulative that even seeing her beaten to a damn pulp still seemed suspicious to me, but something just didn't feel right. I walked down to the cafeteria to grab a cup of coffee and clear my head before heading back upstairs.

Back on Alana's floor, I walked over to a seat near her room and sat down. I pulled out my cell phone to call Alana's mom when a man in a white lab coat approached me. He looked like a doctor.

"Are you Mr. Brooks?" said he asked as I looked up at him.

"Excuse me?"

"Are you the husband of Alana Brooks?"

I paused, wondering if I should say, "Yes." I didn't know why, but I figured I should. "Yes, um, I am," I said with a straight face.

"I'm Dr. Morgan. I'm treating your wife."

"Right, um, so how is she?" I asked.

"She's going to pull through, although I do have some concerns."

Hearing that made me think that Alana's injuries were worse than they looked.

"Has your wife ever tried to hurt herself before in the past?" he asked.

His statement threw me and I was definitely confused. "I'm sorry, I'm not quite following you," I said, as I was becoming even more attentive than before.

"Your wife claims that she was mugged but her wounds clearly indicate that they were self inflicted," Dr. Morgan continued.

"What?"

"Unfortunately," he added, "we see a few of these cases each year."

I looked away and in that moment everything seemed crystal clear. She did it again, I thought, I cannot believe I continue to get sucked back in by her. My mind began to race, and I felt myself become very irritated and annoyed.

"So are you saying that my wife beat herself up on purpose?"

"Yes, but she did it for a reason, and the question is for what reason. Usually when this happens it's the patient's way of crying out for something, usually attention that they feel they are not getting. Would you happen to know what that could be?" Dr. Morgan asked.

I thought for a moment as he waited patiently for me to answer. I slowly shook my head "no," even though I knew exactly what it was. It was me.

"No, I, um, I don't know," I said.

"Well, I recommend psychiatric treatment. Your wife is at least mildly delusional and in need of some help," Dr. Morgan said as he flipped through Alana's chart. "There is a psychiatric ward in the hospital that I can suggest for treatment."

I was silent. This was someone I thought I knew for over 20 years, but apparently I had been wrong. I didn't know this woman at all.

"Are you OK?" Dr. Morgan asked, pulling me out of my trance. "I know this is hard to hear, but believe me, it is for the best, for your wife and her wellbeing."

"Yeah, yeah, I'm fine. Whatever help she needs, please…"

"Good, I'm glad we are on the same page," Dr. Morgan continued.

Maybe this was a blessing in disguise, I thought, a way to get Alana out of my life so I can start a new one with Kai. Funny how things happen, but right now it couldn't be more perfect. "Listen," I said, "do you need me to sign anything to get her admitted as soon as possible?"

"Yes, if you head over to the nurses' station they will get you started on the paperwork."

I stood up, looking eye to eye with Dr. Morgan. "About how long will my wife be in this facility?" I asked.

"We keep our patients for a maximum of three days, then after that they are evaluated by the Treatment Committee that determines if they are stable enough to be released. Of course, a family member can recommend a longer stay at that time, but it really is up to the facility."

"So basically, Alana will be in the facility for three days tops." I said.

"Correct, unless we see that she is a risk to herself or others."

"I see."

I pulled out my business card. "Please, give me a call when that evaluation comes up, I would like to be considered in that decision."

"Will do."

"Thank you doctor, this was very informative," I said as the doctor walked away and I pulled out my cell phone to call Alana's mother. Riley would be living with her for a while, I thought.

After getting everything all squared away with Riley, I headed to the nurses' station to start the paperwork, which would put Alana away for the weekend at least.

It was way past time to head to New York and live the life I was meant to live.

***

I knew I needed to act fast concerning Alana. After signing all the papers to commit her to the psychiatric ward I headed down to the courthouse to get a restraining order put on her. I figured once she realizes what I had done she would be coming after me and this time I wasn't going to wait for anything crazy to happen. I headed out the courthouse, called the airlines and within 12 hours I was on a plane to New York City.

It was hard to contain my excitement as I headed out of JFK and made my way to Brooklyn. I knew

Kai wasn't expecting me for a few days, so I hoped this sudden surprise was the right thing to do. As I rode in the cab, my hands became very sweaty and I started to feel a sense of doubt come over me, as if something wasn't quite right. I took a deep breath and tried to throw out the negative thoughts from my mind and just focus on all the positives that were there to be had. I focused on the buildings of the city as we made our way towards my destination, Fort Green, Brooklyn, and I began to practice what I wanted to say to Kai in my head.

I told myself that I was not going to think about Alana, she had made her bed and now she would have to lie in it. One thing I had to do before I left was call Riley and say goodbye, and tell her that I had to go away for a while. I knew that was never a great thing to hear as a child, but I had to make a decision that was best for Kai and me.

My cab pulled in front of Kai's place and I paid the driver, collected my bags out of the trunk and walked up to the front steps of her brownstone. I couldn't believe all that had happened to finally bring me there, to New York, to a newborn son. Life is crazy, I thought, and you just have to roll with the punches sometimes. I took the last few steps up to the door, stopped for a moment to take a deep breath hoping what I was doing was the right thing. I believed I was. I reached out and rang the doorbell.

***

I had just laid Kristopher down before crawling into the tub for a reprieve. I knew I had at least a couple hours before I was called to duty once again, so I took advantage of every minute. Todd and Toni were on my mind and I was still so confused as to what to do with my life and with them. I loved Todd, but I felt very comfortable with Toni. Simone was right, I had to think about what was best for my son and follow my heart.

Then in that moment of despair, I thought about what my mother always used to tell me, to be careful about mixing up your feelings. She always told me that just because you care deeply for someone doesn't mean you are in love. "Your heart will never lie," she had told me, "and that is what you have to follow."

I let out a loud sigh. I definitely needed a sign, a sign to tell me that I was doing the right thing. My doorbell rang and I opened my eyes. I wasn't expecting anyone and I knew Toni was at a lecture. I quickly got out of the tub, toweled off and grabbed my robe. I slowly walked to the front door and opened it.

I could not believe what I was seeing. It was Todd. I had not been expecting him for a few more days, but the instant I saw him, I knew. I knew he was the one, and all the doubt and all the wondering was gone and I knew exactly what I needed to do.

I threw my arms around him and whispered in his ear, "I'm so glad you're here. I cannot wait to spend the rest of my life with you." I hugged Todd tightly, and knew that nothing would ever come between us again… I hoped.

THE END

EPILOGUE

Todd relinquishes his law practice in Chicago, and he and Kai move to New York where he opens a small but successful practice in Brooklyn. They rent a brownstone of their own, not too far from where Kai was originally living. Kai quits her job and becomes a stay at home mom.

Toni and Kai's friendship understandably fades as Toni continues to teach at NYU where she meets another female and starts a relationship.

Jessica eventually moves back to New York after several failed attempts to sway Alana back into her life.

After Alana is released from the mental hospital 5 days after Todd secretly admitted her, she flees to New York with much rage and resentment. However, her attempts to get Todd back are met with a restraining order that Alana does not obey; her one last act of defiance quickly lands her in jail for 3 years.

****

COMING IN 2013

ALANA BITES BACK (Book 3)
It's not over until Alana says it is

Could Alana be done for good or will she seek out her own revenge after her release from jail? Find out in the 3rd installment of My Man's Best Friend in book 3: ALANA BITES BACK.

Also coming in 2013 a new novel by K. Elle Collier:

<u>Intimate Stranger</u>

Just how well do you know the person sleeping next to you?

For updates, book giveaways and release dates of my upcoming novels, visit me at:

<u>www.kellecollier.com</u>

Thank you for your purchase ☒. If you liked what you read, please leave a kind review on Amazon.com

About the Author:

K. Elle Collier started her writing career off by participating in various esteemed writing programs such as: The Bill Cosby writing Workshop, The Walt Disney Writing Fellowship as well as Warner Bros. Comedy Writing Program, this in turn lead to a staff writing position on the CW sitcom Girlfriends. K. Elle later branched off to other avenues of writing such as screenplays and stage plays, where she adapted the best-selling novel 'Friends and Lovers' by Eric Jerome Dickey for the stage. 'Kai's Aftermath' is the sequel to 'My Man's Best Friend'. K. Elle lives in Los Angeles California.

3.3
33
33
23
23
───────
1.45

Made in the USA
San Bernardino, CA
24 April 2015